"I had to come h
and figure out w
for the rest of my ~~~~ **Alyssa.**

"And you came up with being a private investigator?"

"For now, it works. I'm my own boss, and I can use my training."

"Your special skills? Like beating up thugs in skeleton masks and escaping from a second-story warehouse window and tearing up the streets with your evasive driving? An interesting collection of talent, but I've got to admit that you're good at what you do."

"Merci."

"I'm guessing there's something else driving you. You're not a pirate—you're a hero. I think you enjoy helping people like me, doing the right thing."

Again, he shrugged. "I like being able to choose which jobs to take and which to turn down."

"Why did you choose me?"

"For the challenge. Besides, all the positions for knights in shining armor were filled."

WITNESS
ON THE RUN

USA TODAY Bestselling Author
CASSIE MILES

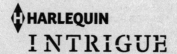

HARLEQUIN
INTRIGUE

To Carla Gertner for her inspiration and knowledge of
New Orleans and, as always, to Rick.

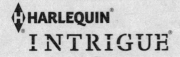

INTRIGUE

Recycling programs
for this product may
not exist in your area.

ISBN-13: 978-1-335-13590-2

Witness on the Run

Copyright © 2020 by Kay Bergstrom

This edition published by arrangement with Harlequin Books S.A.

For questions and comments about the quality of this book,
please contact us at CustomerService@Harlequin.com.

Harlequin Enterprises ULC
22 Adelaide St. West, 40th Floor
Toronto, Ontario M5H 4E3, Canada
www.Harlequin.com

Printed in U.S.A.

Cassie Miles, a *USA TODAY* bestselling author, lives in Colorado. After raising two daughters and cooking tons of macaroni and cheese for her family, Cassie is trying to be more adventurous in her culinary efforts. She's discovered that almost anything tastes better with wine. When she's not plotting Harlequin Intrigue books, Cassie likes to hang out at the Denver Botanic Gardens near her high-rise home.

Books by Cassie Miles

Harlequin Intrigue

Mountain Midwife
Sovereign Sheriff
Baby Battalion
Unforgettable
Midwife Cover
Mommy Midwife
Montana Midwife
Hostage Midwife
Mountain Heiress
Snowed In
Snow Blind
Mountain Retreat
Colorado Wildfire
Mountain Bodyguard
Mountain Shelter
Mountain Blizzard
Frozen Memories
The Girl Who Wouldn't Stay Dead
The Girl Who Couldn't Forget
The Final Secret
Witness on the Run

Visit the Author Profile page at Harlequin.com.

CAST OF CHARACTERS

Alyssa Bailey—The twenty-six-year-old accountant for a pawnbroker in Chicago witnesses a murder and is taken into witness protection in New Orleans.

Rafe Fournier—A New Orleans native and descendant from pirates, he is a private investigator who is hired to protect Alyssa.

Viktor Davidoff—Also known as Diamond Jim, Davidoff owns several used-car lots and believes Alyssa is in possession of information he needs.

Max Horowitz—Alyssa's employer in Chicago, the pawnbroker disappears after the murder.

Hugh Woodbridge—A US marshal working for WITSEC, he betrays his duty to go after Alyssa.

Chapter One

The Day of the Dead celebration unleashed a parade of floats, bands, ghosts, skeletons and zombies that wended through the night in the French Quarter of New Orleans. Some people carried tiki torches while others waved neon lights. Alyssa Bailey stood with a crowd on the curb and watched. The thought of dancing in the street made her self-conscious. She had turned in her ledgers and calculator three years ago when she first entered the witness protection program, but she still had the soul of a quiet accountant who liked to have every *i* dotted and every *t* crossed.

This year, she vowed, would be different. No more standing on the sidelines. She was twenty-seven and needed to join the parade before life passed her by. During *Día de los Muertos* on the weekend after Halloween, the veil between the real world and the afterlife thinned. The dead craved laughter, song and revelry. Alyssa was determined to get into the spirit of the thing.

Just before she got off work at half past nine, she'd gotten a phone call from someone anonymous saying they'd see her at the parade. The voice had been so garbled that she couldn't tell if the caller was male or female, but she intended to keep a lookout for a familiar face.

Gathering her courage, she took a giant step into the street, where she shuffled along to the irresistible beat of drums and death rattles. Her eardrums popped when the trumpets and saxophones wailed. People in crazy costumes bumped and jostled. She told herself that this was fun, fun, fun but didn't believe it. The wild display of neon, color and confetti made her feel like she was inside a raucous, whirling kaleidoscope.

A masked ghost dressed like an 1800s pirate approached her, whipped off his tricorn hat and swept a bow before he grasped her hands and spun her in a circle. The music shifted gears from a dirge to a more upbeat tempo, and her pirate led her in an energetic dance that was half waltz, half polka and one hundred percent exciting—more thrilling than the handful of dates she'd had in the last three years.

He leaned close and said, "Tell me about your costume. Who are you?"

She'd put together a ragged outfit of pantaloons and an old-fashioned gown with a low bodice, lace trim and a tattered skirt. The clothes were meant to honor her mother. Mom had been born and raised in Savannah. Though they'd lived in Chicago for as long as Alyssa could remember, her mom would always be a southern belle. Five years ago, she'd been killed in a hit-and-run.

Tilting her head, she gazed up at her pirate's silver half mask. Though she couldn't see his eyes, his mouth was visible. He had a divot in his chin—very sexy. She swallowed hard and said, "I'm supposed to be a zombie Scarlett O'Hara."

"Good choice, *cher*. With your dark hair and green eyes, you make a real pretty Scarlett."

Her mom had always said the same. "Did you call me?" she asked. "Was I supposed to meet you here at the parade?"

"We didn't have an appointment."

"Well, we should have." Alyssa gestured to his white shirt with full sleeves and his burgundy velvet vest with gold buttons. "Are you a famous pirate? Jean Lafitte?"

Again, he doffed the hat and bowed. "I'm the ghost of Captain Jean-Pierre Fournier, an original pirate of the Caribbean and one of my ancestors. I am Rafael Fournier."

"I do declare," she said in a corny southern accent. Unaccustomed to teasing, she wasn't sure she was doing it right. "I'm ever so pleased to make your acquaintance, Rafael."

"*Enchanté, mademoiselle.* Please call me Rafe."

He twirled her again and then held her close. Their posture felt strangely intimate in the midst of a wild crowd. Her half-exposed breasts crushed against his firm chest. Their thighs touched. He guided her so skillfully that she felt graceful, beautiful and sultry. Before she knew what was happening, they were dancing a tango. *A tango? No way!* She didn't know these steps but must have been doing something right. People in the crowd made way for them and applauded as they passed by.

When their dance ended, he dropped a kiss on her forehead. "*Merci, ma belle.*"

With a flourish, he disappeared into the crowd—an impressive feat for a guy who was over six feet tall with wide shoulders and puffy sleeves. He'd kissed her and called her *belle*, beautiful. *Moi?*

Their dance gave her courage. Life was meant to be celebrated. When a laughing zombie placed a beer in her hand, Alyssa took a huge gulp and wholeheartedly threw herself into the parade, bounding along the street, snapping her fingers and shaking her hips. Her mom would have loved this scene. If she were here, she'd have danced all night. It was Alyssa's duty to celebrate in Mom's place, dancing with pirates and looking for mysterious people who left anonymous messages.

On a street corner, she encountered a guy dressed like Baron Samedi, the voodoo master of the dead, with a skull face and top hat. He blew a puff of chalky powder at the crowd, making everybody more ghostlike. All around her, people were laughing and waving, drinking and dancing. New Orleans took every opportunity to party—from Mardi Gras to funeral processions to *Día de los Muertos*.

Dodging around a dour threesome in skull masks, she joined a group of zombie belly dancers with tambourines. A four-member band played "When the Saints Go Marching In," and she sang with loud enthusiasm that was hugely out of character. She danced along a street where the storefronts were mostly voodoo shops. The fortune tellers stood outside, enticing tourists with offers of special deals. For a small fee, the bereaved could have a conversation with loved ones who had crossed over. Instead of dismissing the voodoo promises as illogical and absurd, Alyssa imagined how wonderful it would be to talk to Mom one more time.

A loud, raucous laugh cut through the music. Alyssa knew that sound. A shiver prickled between her shoulder blades, as quick and creepy as a spider running across her back. She peered toward the fortune tellers on the sidewalk. Amid the crowd, she saw a woman who looked like her mother. She stood in a doorway, laughing with her head thrown back and her long silver hair rising in a cloud of curls around her head.

Could it be? Her mom couldn't be the voice on the phone. Alyssa would have recognized her. And she was dead, very dead—Alyssa had identified the remains. She caught another glimpse. The silver-haired woman looked so much like her mom. Could she be a ghost?

Alyssa broke away from the parade and ran toward the place where she'd seen the woman. A trombone player got in her way, and then a high-kicking can-can dancer. The music shifted to a minor key as a feeling of dread swelled in her chest and spread through her body. The shop where the woman had been standing was closed, and the door was locked.

Frantically, Alyssa asked if anyone had seen her. Nobody knew anything. Nor did they care. *Laissez les bon temps rouler*—let the good times roll.

But Alyssa couldn't let go. The woman's resemblance to her mom was too uncanny to ignore. Operating on instinct, she darted through an alley and came out on a street where there weren't as many people. She crossed at the stoplight and entered a park with a large brick patio and bronze statues of jazz legends. Pacing back and forth, she scanned in all directions.

At the edge of a grassy area lined with fat palm trees she saw the three men in matching skeleton masks who had been at the parade. She'd noticed their cold, serious attitude. Why were they here? Had they followed her?

The tallest asked, "Do you need help?"

"I'm looking for a woman. She has curly silver hair."

"Oh yeah, we saw her. Come with us."

The three of them surrounded her. She was trapped and beginning to be scared. "Forget about it. I'm sorry I bothered you."

He edged closer. "You're coming with us."

For the three years that she'd been in the witness protection program, she'd lived in fear of this moment. The dangerous criminals she'd testified against wanted to take revenge, and she figured that it was only a matter of time before they found her. She pivoted on her heel, tried to run.

The leader grabbed her arm and yanked. The other two closed in. One of them slapped a cloth over her mouth to keep her from calling for help.

She couldn't breathe. A sickly-sweet antiseptic smell penetrated her nostrils. She heard the men in skeleton masks laughing, telling witnesses that she'd had too much to drink and they'd make sure she got home.

She struggled, kicked at their legs and lashed out with her arms. She clawed at one of the skeleton masks, and it came off in her hands. She found herself staring into flat, dark eyes above a sneering mouth and hatchet jaw. A cruel face—this man would show no mercy.

Her vision blurred. She was losing her grip on consciousness.

In half-awake glimpses, she saw another man come closer and shove one of the skeletons. It was her pirate. He demanded they release her. She tried to warn him that these were violent men, but her throat closed. She couldn't make a sound. The pirate attacked the others. She thought he had a stun gun but really couldn't tell.

When the skeleton let go of her arm, she fell onto the grass and desperately crawled. Her head was spinning. Her body was numb. She had to escape. One of the skeletons kicked her. She barely felt the pain.

Alyssa staggered to her feet, concentrated on putting one foot in front of the other. Her legs were rubber bands, incapable of supporting her. She fell again.

The next thing she knew, she'd been flung over someone's shoulder and was being carried. She attempted to wriggle free but couldn't move. Her last reserve of strength drained from her, and she went limp. She was caught. They had her. She hoped it wouldn't hurt too much when they killed her.

She was dumped into a car seat. Someone reached across to fasten her seat belt. Forcing her eyes open, she saw the dashing pirate. He had come to her rescue. *Merci, Captain Fournier.*

Chapter Two

Alyssa woke with a gasp. Her eyes snapped open. *Where am I?*

It appeared that she was in her bedroom, lying flat on her back with her arms tucked straight down at her sides under her vintage chenille bedspread. A small lamp with a glass base and fringed shade cast a soft circle of light on the bedside table. She saw her music box with the twirling ballerina inside—a gift from her father.

Still night—it was dark around the edges of the window blinds. What time was it? Gazing across the dimly lit bedroom, she tried to read the red digital numbers on the alarm clock that stood on her dresser, but she couldn't see it. How did she get home? She remembered the parade, *Día de los Muertos*. There had been dancing, and she'd seen the ghost of her mom before she was attacked by skeletons. *Was it a nightmare? A dream?* Her thoughts disintegrated into static.

Hoping to ground herself in reality, she turned her head and looked toward the music box. When the lid opened, the tinkling music would play "Lara's Theme" from *Dr. Zhivago*, which was perfect because Lara was her real name. She hadn't been allowed to bring photos when she entered WitSec, but she'd refused to leave the precious music box behind. Her father was long gone. She couldn't remember what he looked like and had never known his name, but he'd loved her enough to give her this present on her fourth birthday. Small reassurance, but it was better than nothing.

She realized that her cell phone wasn't on the bedside table. Matter of fact, the charger wasn't there, either. *Strange.* She *always* charged her phone at night. The only thing on the table other than her music box was a cut-glass bowl of her homemade potpourri. She inhaled a whiff. The familiar scents of orange, cinnamon and vanilla should have comforted her, but she was growing more anxious by the minute. Her bedroom felt oddly foreign. She peered through the shadows at the Toulouse-Lautrec print on the wall opposite her bed—a can-can dancer at the Moulin Rouge. She'd picked it out herself. Of course, she was home.

Focus, I need to focus. The music box looked different, less battered. When she pulled her arm from under the covers and reached for the box, she saw a swelling on her upper arm, the beginning of a bruise, and a bandage wrapped around her wrist. When she touched the bandage, she felt a stinging sensation. That wasn't her only pain. As soon as she moved, she experienced a pulsing headache. Her ribs throbbed. Lowering the bedspread, she looked down at the bruises on her side and gauze bandages on her knees. She was wearing nothing but her black sports bra and silky blue panties.

Sitting upright on the bed, she held the music box. Seeking comfort from a familiar object, her fingers stroked the worn wooden edges of her talisman—a souvenir of another time, another home, another life. She lifted the lid. The delicate ballerina pirouetted on tiptoe, and the jingly music played "Twinkle, Twinkle Little Star." Not her tune! Not her music box!

The door swung open. A man strode into her bedroom.

More outraged than frightened, she demanded, "Who are you? What are you doing in my house?"

"Not to worry, *cher*. You'll understand as soon as I turn on the light."

The overhead light erased the shadows. Her gaze slid across the walls. The window was in the wrong place. Her shabby chic furniture had been replaced with stuff that was plain old shabby. *Not my house!* "Where am I?"

He took a step toward her. "You have no cause for alarm. I can explain."

"Stop where you are. Don't come any closer."

But the stranger took another step, murmuring about how she was safe. She didn't believe him, not for a minute. With as much force as she could muster, she threw the music box at him. It crashed against the wall.

Though logic told her that this wasn't really her bedroom, she struggled free from the blankets, climbed out of bed and ripped open the drawer to the bedside table where she kept her snub-nose Smith & Wesson .38. The drawer was empty. She snatched the bowl filled with dried, scented leaves and drew back her arm to throw it.

The stranger held up a hand to stop her. "Wait!"

She hesitated. "Why does this bedroom look like mine?"

"It's all right, *cher.*" He offered a disarming smile. "Put down the bowl. You don't want to break it and get glass on the floor. No, no, *ma chérie.* Step away from the potpourri."

As soon as he spoke, she realized the absurdity. Dried leaves weren't a lethal weapon.

And he wasn't wrong. Breaking the bowl would make a mess. "Where am I?"

"Nothing to worry about," he said. "Don't you recognize me?"

His face seemed familiar, and he was so appealing that she wanted to believe he meant no harm. But Alyssa wasn't a fool. She needed to figure out who this charming Frenchman was and what she needed to do next. "This is the last time I'm going to ask. Where the hell am I?"

He rattled off an address. "That's about six miles northeast of the French Quarter."

"How did I get here?" A sliver of memory pierced her mind. She recalled being carried and placed into an SUV. Her seat belt had been fastened by the man who rescued her—the man who now stood on the opposite side of the room. "You—you're my pirate."

"Rafe Fournier." His sweeping bow was far less effective when he wasn't wearing the swashbuckler's costume. Jeans and a black T-shirt weren't dramatic. "At your service, *ma belle.*"

She should have recognized him sooner with his subtly accented voice and sexy grin, but he'd been masked from the nose up. She warned him, "You shouldn't have gotten involved. This isn't your fight, and those men are dangerous."

"They're cowards. Any man who lays hands on a woman needs to be taught a lesson."

Very gallant but not real bright—he could have been killed. When she shook her head, the pain ratcheted up a few notches, and she regretted leaping from the bed. Her entire body was stiff and sore. The inside of her mouth tasted like cotton. Physically, she felt miserable, but her brain was beginning to sort out the details. Fact: Rafe had appeared in the nick of time. Fact: He knew a lot about her. Fact: He had created a duplicate of her bedroom. *Very suspicious!* "You were following me, weren't you?"

"This explanation is going to take a while. Why don't you settle down and rest?"

As her mind cleared, she came to the obvious realization that she was nearly naked. She dragged the chenille spread off the bed, wrapped it around her and draped the fabric over her shoulder like a toga. "Why did you take my clothes off?"

"Accept my apology, *s'il vous plaît.* I needed to treat your cuts and scrapes and make sure you didn't need medical attention."

A rational explanation, but she wasn't about to let him off the hook. "Where's my stuff?"

"In the closet." He pointed to a closed door. "Everything is there, except your cell phone, which I am charging in the kitchen."

Intending to grab her clothes and get out of this crazy, through-the-looking-glass bedroom, she stumbled toward the closet and made it all the way to the foot of the bed before a wave of vertigo overwhelmed her. She stood still until she'd regained her balance. When he moved toward her, she snapped, "Don't come any closer."

"You don't trust me," he said.

"Damn right, I don't!" His timely appearance when she was attacked might be part of a larger scheme. She'd never believed in coincidence.

"You're dehydrated." Several plastic bottles of water stood atop the dresser. He grabbed one and tossed it onto the bed. "Drink."

Cautiously, she picked up the bottle. The cap was still fastened, which meant he hadn't tampered with the contents. Taking a few sips shouldn't be dangerous. She raised the bottle to her lips. The cool liquid moistened the interior of her mouth and slid down her throat. After another sip, she felt marginally improved. "Tastes good."

"Have some more. The liquid will dilute whatever is in your system. If you like I can give you something for the pain."

"Do you really think I'm dumb enough to accept mystery meds from somebody I just met? For all I know, you could be the one who drugged me in the first place."

"Do you remember being drugged?"

"Not very well." But she knew that Rafe wasn't responsible. She recalled a cloth being pressed over her mouth and the antiseptic smell of whatever chemical formula had knocked her out. "There were three skeletons. I can't remember how I got all these bruises."

"You were attacked, three against one."

"Who were they? What else did you see?"

"Not much. I got you away from them, put you in my car and brought you here." He folded his arms across his torso and leaned his shoulder against the door frame. "It's your turn to speak, *cher*. Tell me what you remember."

Though grateful to him for helping her out, she didn't owe Rafe an explanation. "Why do you want to know?"

He pursed his lips and gave a very Gallic shrug. "If we share information, we might understand who those men were and why they attacked."

His logic made sense. If she could figure out the names of her attackers, she'd know what to do to evade them. Leaving the investigation to WitSec was also logical, but the marshals weren't likely to share details with her. Rafe was offering her a chance to face the threat. There was no harm in talking to him. "What do you want to know? Where should I start?"

"The beginning."

"I got off work at the bistro at half past nine."
Don't say too much! Before she even got started,
she was throwing up mental roadblocks. She
stumbled backward and braced herself against
the bedroom wall. To her immediate left was a
window. Peeking through the blinds, she saw
that they were on the first floor. *I should get out
of here. It's time to run.*

"Are you all right?"

She picked up her narrative. "In the employees' locker room, I changed into my costume.
At first, I wasn't sure I'd go to the parade, but I
got a phone call from somebody who said they'd
meet me."

"Who called you?"

"Anonymous," she said. "Nothing showed up
on caller ID, but I took it as a sign that I should
go and try to have fun."

"Did you know the voice?"

"No." The phone message could have been
a trap. The men in skeleton masks might have
been luring her. But how did they know her
phone number? Who were they? From the street
outside, she heard the clang of a streetcar. "It
could have been a man or a woman with a low
voice. It could have been you."

"But it wasn't."

"Almost as soon as I joined the parade, you approached me. Why?"

"I promise, *cher*, to tell you as much of the story as I can. But first, I've got to hear your recollections. Details might help the cops find the bad guys."

"No police."

In situations like this where her cover might be blown, the protocol required her to report to WitSec. She should make that call right now, and yet something held her back. The attack had warped her perceptions. She wasn't sure who could be trusted. And how could she make that determination?

After another drink of water, she scrutinized Rafe. When she was first taken into protective custody and the marshals started asking questions, she'd gotten good at describing the criminals she'd encountered in Chicago. She formulated an analysis of Rafe. His height was about six feet two or three, and he probably weighed 185 or 190 pounds. The dimple in his square chin counted as a distinguishing feature. Other than that, he was a standard version of handsome with wavy brown hair, gray eyes and a smile that could melt your heart.

Those were the physical details, and they didn't help her decide if he was trustworthy. "I remember our tango," she said.

"We fit together well."

"After you vanished into the crowd, I joined a group of belly dancers with tambourines. We were clapping and dancing, and I sang along with them."

"You have a strong voice. Not a good voice, but strong."

"Did you hear me singing? Were you watching me?"

"Always, *cher.*"

He sounded like a stalker. "Do you make a habit of following me around?"

"I usually know where you are. You stick to a regular routine."

The marshals in WitSec had warned her not to be so predictable. She was supposed to take different routes to work and to shop at different supermarkets. At first, she'd followed their rules. But after a while, she established her own itinerary for handling danger. It might be time to put her plans into effect.

She finished the water and lobbed the empty plastic bottle onto the bed. "I'd like another, please. And I need my phone."

If she decided to notify WitSec, her life in New Orleans was over. She didn't relish the idea of starting over in another city, but that was the deal. She did what they told her, and they kept her protected…except for tonight. Somebody had fumbled the ball.

Without coming too close, Rafe dropped another bottle onto the bed. When she picked it up, he held out a small container of nonprescription painkillers. "The seal is intact," he said. "You can see that I didn't touch the pills."

Grateful, she took the container. After fumbling with the childproof lid, she shook out three capsules and gulped them down. Though still in pain, she felt better than when she'd bolted from the bed, more in control. "About that phone?"

"How long were you singing with the belly dancers?"

"A couple of blocks. Then we moved into that area with voodoo shops." And she'd heard her mom's laugh. "There was a silver-haired woman on the sidewalk. Did you see her?"

He nodded. "An attractive woman wearing dozens of shiny Mardi Gras necklaces."

"She looked so much like my mom that I had to find her, had to talk to her. Even though I knew it couldn't be Mom. She died five years ago. Her name was Claudia."

"I know," Rafe said.

"How do you know her name?"

"I know a great deal about you. Continue with your story. What happened next?"

"I ran in the direction I thought the woman

might have gone, went into that park, then the guys in skeleton masks surrounded me. I never should have let them get so close. When they grabbed me, I clawed at one of the masks. It came off in my hand."

"Did you see his face?"

"Yes."

"Did you recognize him?"

"No." But she'd seen that heavy jaw before. His empty, soulless eyes would haunt her nightmares.

"Maybe," he said, "maybe you're remembering, maybe just a little piece. Was his hair blond or brown?"

It seemed wise to keep her secrets to herself. "I don't know."

"I want you to look at mug shots."

Though Rafe hadn't moved a whit, his attitude transformed from casual street pirate to alert professional. "You sound like a cop."

"Good guess, *cher*. A while back, I used to be in the FBI."

"And now?"

"Private detective," he said. "Two and a half weeks ago, I was hired to keep an eye on you."

She sat on the edge of the bed and drank more water. "Who hired you?"

"I can't give you a name, but I can assure you that my client means you no harm."

She wished she could believe this tall, handsome, gray-eyed man, but life had taught her not to give her trust so easily. The price for naivety was steep. She came at the question of his client's identity from a different angle. "Did this mystery person tell you to decorate this room like my house?"

"My client thought the similarity in the room might make you more comfortable."

"Why would anybody think that? I'm not a child who needs her favorite toys, especially not the music box. It played the wrong tune, you know."

"Duly noted," he said. "My client wanted you to feel at home."

"Why would that matter? I have no intention of staying here." Anger sparked inside her. "You didn't think you could keep me locked in this room, did you?"

"I did not."

A horrible thought occurred to her. "How do you know what my bedroom looks like? Did you sneak into my house?"

"I avoid breaking the law whenever possible."

"Did you take pictures?"

"Photos were taken."

And if he didn't enter her house, how did he take pictures? Did he use a drone? Or dangle from a tree outside the window? "You spied on me. Like a Peeping Tom."

"I was careful to respect your privacy."

How could she believe him? The first chance he got, he'd stripped off her clothes. His rationale of treating her injuries made sense, but it was still a violation. "You said you were hired two and a half weeks ago—"

"Sixteen days," he said.

"And you've been watching me ever since. You know what I call that? Stalking. You're a damn stalker."

"Not stalking," he said, "protecting."

"Why?"

He shrugged. "It's my job to keep you safe."

If that were true, he shouldn't have any objection to contacting the WitSec offices. *Make the call!* She was angry and, at the same time, exhausted. She scooted back against the pillows and pulled the bedspread over her body. "What if I said I wanted to leave? Would you let me walk out the door?"

"Of course, but you might want to take a moment—while the assault is still fresh in your mind—to figure out who is after you. Who was the man behind the skeleton mask?"

"Why should I tell you?"

"We're on the same team. I can help you. I learned techniques in the FBI to jump-start your memory." His voice was gentle and cajoling, so charming. "We can try a few simple concentration techniques. You're smart, *cher*. You'll remember."

"Leave me alone."

"Allow yourself to relax. Close your eyes."

Though she didn't agree to cooperate, her eyelids slammed shut. She believed in meditation and was good at controlling her breathing. While he continued to talk in soothing tones, she focused. In her mind, she saw the face of the man who attacked her. Ignoring the terror she'd felt, she waited until his features became clear. With sandy hair and cold dark eyes, he was average-looking, except for his hatchet-shaped jaw. His mouth was wide, and he had big teeth, horse teeth. *I know him.* She didn't have a name or a title, but she'd seen him at the WitSec offices. The man behind the skeleton mask was a US marshal.

Her body tensed under the covers. Her subconscious mind had been protecting her. That was why she didn't call WitSec. She couldn't trust the marshals—couldn't trust anyone.

Rafe encouraged her. "Tell me. You figured something out."

If she was straightforward with him, she doubted that he'd let her walk out the door. *Trust no one.* The only way she'd escape was to make a run for it. She gave a huge, deliberate yawn. "I need to sleep. You should leave."

"We have more to talk about, *cher*."

"Not now...too tired. Please turn off the light and close the door."

She heard the click of the switch for the overhead light. Darkness descended. Opening her eyes a slit, she saw the circle of light on the bedside table where the music box had been.

He lowered his voice to an intimate whisper. "Sleep well, *cher*."

The door closed, and he was gone.

Chapter Three

Outside the bedroom door, Rafe walked down the short hallway toward the bathroom with a purposely heavy tread. He figured Alyssa would be lying in the bed and listening—waiting until he was out of the way before she made her move, which, he suspected, would be to run away by sneaking down this hallway or climbing out the window. Though he wanted to believe that she'd rest for a while and then wake up and have a reasonable conversation, he doubted that would happen. She didn't trust him. Nothing he said or did would make her think differently.

For the past couple of weeks while he'd been observing Alyssa, he had developed a pretty good idea what to expect from her. Her sweet, bashful attitude was genuine, but this pretty lady could also be as stubborn and immovable as a block of granite. When she made up her mind to do something, she carried through. If she successfully managed to disappear, she'd be hard to catch, especially since she already distrusted him.

Someone else might have better luck convincing Alyssa to cooperate. Another woman could reassure her and let her know that Rafe was on her side. In the kitchen of the very small house, he made a call to a confidential informant he'd worked with for many years. Sheila Marie knew everybody in New Orleans and heard every rumor. Her connections stretched from the parish courthouse to the voodoo dens in the bayous to the wild parties in the French Quarter.

His CI answered after two rings. "Rafe, you pretty man, why you calling me?"

The strains of a jazzy saxophone wailed in the background. "Sounds like you're celebrating the Day of the Dead."

"Where you at? I expected to see you parading like your pirate uncle. Did I ever tell you about the day I saw naughty Jean-Pierre himself peep over your shoulder? And I heard his rumbling voice. He be liking you better as a gumshoe than a fed."

Sometimes it was handy to have an informant who talked to ghosts. "I have an assignment for you."

"Sure 'nuff."

"I'm looking for someone who was at the parade, near Jolene's gris-gris shop. This woman is tall and skinny and has curly silver hair. She's in her sixties."

"Prime of life," Sheila Marie said. "I'll ask around."

"And if I need help from you later tonight?"

"I'm at Becca's Bar on Canal."

He truly appreciated her help. "You are *magnifique*."

"Betcha say that to all the ladies."

"Only you, Sheila Marie."

He put away his phone. Stepping lightly, he returned to the bedroom door and leaned against the wall beside it, lurking and listening. Alyssa was half right when she called him a stalker. Much of his work as a PI or an undercover FBI agent involved sneaking around in the shadows, hiding behind other identities and lying. The difference between him and a run-of-the-mill Peeping Tom was that Rafe didn't get a buzz from watching.

He wanted to tell Alyssa the truth, but the time wasn't right, and he wasn't altogether sure this lady could be trusted. His investigation into her background had uncovered some potentially unusual maneuvering with finances. He knew she had at least one fake passport. And she kept two safe-deposit boxes in different banks.

Tonight, she hadn't told outright lies but had been misleading. Most suspicious was her reluctance to call WitSec. That should have been the first thing she did when she regained consciousness. If she'd insisted upon making that contact, his mission would have become even more complicated, but Alyssa never even mentioned witness protection.

Maybe she didn't believe the marshals could keep her safe. Given the events of this evening, he couldn't fault that opinion. Those masked skeletons were clumsy in their approach, but they'd known where she'd be. One of them might have made the anonymous phone call encouraging her to come to the parade.

From behind the closed door, he heard the bedsprings creak. In bare feet, her movements were a nearly silent shuffle, but he could tell when she turned the knob and opened the closet door. He hadn't left her defenseless when it came to clothing. Not only had he draped her Scarlett O'Hara rags on a hanger, but he'd added a couple of his own shirts and a pair of gym shorts that would undoubtedly be too big for her. In a pocket of her Scarlett pantaloons, he'd found a slim wallet with a couple of bucks, identification and a credit card. There was also a key chain with a fob and four keys. Though he left those things in her possession, he'd scanned every bit of her stuff until he was dead certain that nothing was bugged. The only item he'd taken was her cell phone, which he'd disabled so her location couldn't be traced.

When he brought her here, he made sure they weren't followed. The security he had arranged at this location was similar to an FBI safe house with alarms, surveillance cameras and sensors. If she opened a door or a window without his authorization, he'd be alerted by a silent alarm. None of his electronics rang through to the police. Rafe didn't want to share his secret safe house with the authorities or anybody else, not even the man who'd hired him.

There were a couple of thuds from inside the bedroom, and he heard her curse under her breath. Getting dressed in the dark shouldn't be that difficult unless she'd decided to put on that old-fashioned corset, which had been complicated and utterly unnecessary for a woman like her. Alyssa didn't need to cinch her waist. Her natural curves, firm muscles and long legs were spectacular, truly *magnifique*. Her job as a sous chef at the bistro had taken a toll on her hands and forearms, which were reddened and freckled with spots from grease burns. But her midriff felt as sleek as satin. The bruise on her rib cage where she'd been kicked had infuriated

Rafe. There was something deeply wrong about harming such a delicate creature.

Even if he wasn't being paid as a bodyguard, he would have instinctively wanted to protect her. The first step would be to identify her attackers. While she'd been lying on the bed in a meditative state with her eyes closed, he'd seen her fists clench and her brow pull into a scowl. He suspected that she'd been touched by a memory. The skeleton she had unmasked might be somebody she knew from Chicago. Unfortunately, she hadn't chosen to share that information, didn't want to say the name. She didn't trust him.

When he mentioned mug shots, she'd reacted the same way. *No police*, she'd said. Why not? He didn't want to believe that Alyssa was on the wrong side of the many crimes her old boss had committed, but she was a skilled bookkeeper, capable of hiding her involvement in money laundering and fraud.

Her accounting talents had worried Davis James, the man who'd hired Rafe. The client had made a compelling argument about his personal interest in Alyssa and his fear that she might be in danger, but Rafe had smelled a rodent and had used Chance Gregory—a computer genius who occasionally worked for the FBI—to trace his client's background.

Chance uncovered a steaming pile of dirt, starting with his client's name. Davis James was really Viktor Davidoff. He owned six used car lots—Diamond Jim's—in the Chicago area, and he was the alleged boss of a multimillion-dollar international group that specialized in smuggling exotic vehicles. When Davidoff hired Rafe, he'd refused to reveal how he'd learned that Alyssa was in New Orleans. Who had leaked that vital information? Who else knew her location? How were they connected to the men in skeleton masks?

From inside the bedroom, he heard the scratchy noise of the window being gradually raised inch by inch. The alarm system connected to his cell phone messaged him with the same info. Alyssa intended to make her escape that way.

Knowing that she'd need a few minutes to remove the screen and slip outside, he crept down the hallway to the kitchen and out the back door. His lightweight Kawasaki motorcycle was locked in the garage behind the house. For a moment, he considered trailing after her on foot but decided against it. On the bike, he had greater maneuverability and could continue to follow if she hailed a cab.

Taking a position on the breezeway beside the house, he watched her cross the lawn, stumble on a crack in the sidewalk and hide against the trunk of a live oak until there were no headlights on the street. He imagined her heart beating fast and her gaze darting through the night, looking for skeletons and for him. Her outfit was a little bit crazy. His extra-large black Saints T-shirt with a gold fleur-de-lis drooped over her lacy Scarlett pantaloons. On her feet she wore black dancing slippers with two-inch heels and straps.

Chasing her down and dragging her back to the safe house was one option, but he knew Alyssa wouldn't respond to bullying. If he could convince her to trust him, he could keep her safe. And he was curious. A logical, organized person like Alyssa wouldn't forget about Wit-Sec, and she wouldn't rush off into the night without some kind of plan. If he followed, she might lead him somewhere that would explain what she was doing.

When she was almost a block away, he started up his bike and eased into the street. Two blocks away was the streetcar that ran all night on weekends. It was only a little after one o'clock, early for a Saturday. Even in her baggy T-shirt, she wouldn't stand out in a crowd of partying zombies and ghosts from *Día de los Muertos*.

Staying out of sight, he circled the block and found a parking spot where he could see her. He turned off the motor, kept his helmet on and watched as she waited at a stop for the trolley. If she intended to go to her house, she was on the wrong side of the street. Alyssa didn't make careless mistakes, which meant that her escape included a return toward the French Quarter. *An unexpected direction.* Maybe she was heading back to the bistro where she worked, or maybe there was a friend who would give her shelter. Countless possibilities presented themselves.

For sixteen days, he'd managed to watch her without attracting her notice, but now she knew him and could pick him out of a crowd. Surveillance would be ten times harder. He took out his cell phone to arrange for a meet with Sheila Marie. He needed backup.

In the meantime, Rafe would continue to be a stalker.

Chapter Four

Waiting for the streetcar, Alyssa kept to the far side of the sidewalk where a break in the shrubs that lined a wrought iron fence gave her a place to hide. Her entire body hurt. From her head to her rib cage to the palms of her hands and the scratches on her knees, she bristled with pain and tension. Taking another pain pill and falling back to sleep would have been nice, but she didn't have that choice. She had to run. There was no time for slumber—she needed to get away from the danger that had found her in New Orleans.

Though the night was cool, sweat dampened her forehead. She welcomed the sultry breeze that coiled around her bare legs like a torn veil. The mist limited her field of vision and gave her the hopeful illusion that she was invisible. Except for the squeaky window, she'd been quiet when she slipped outside and fled from the house, but that didn't mean Rafe hadn't figured out what she was doing.

She wished she knew who hired him. His refusal to tell her the name of his client worried her. She hated to think he might be working for someone who hated her, someone she'd testified against. Rafe had fought the guys in skeleton masks, so he wasn't connected to them. But he admitted he'd been a fed. Agents from the FBI, like the US Marshals, could be after her. *Why? Has the whole world turned against me?*

Paranoid and in pain, her life was a wreck. Crouching back into the bushes, she scanned the area. Only a few cars rolled under the streetlamps. She didn't see Rafe. Not that she trusted her powers of observation. During the time he'd tracked her, she hadn't noticed a thing. Either he was really good at sneaking around or she was oblivious.

The clang of the trolley alerted her to its approach, and she limped forward so the driver would see her and stop. When she'd first moved here, she'd memorized the streetcar routes. From here, she'd go about a mile and transfer onto the Canal Street line, which would take her close to her destination. After growing up in a big city, she preferred public transportation to the hassle of searching for a parking space. And she enjoyed the New Orleans streetcars. This one was painted a cheerful red with yellow trim. She hopped inside and slid onto a mahogany bench seat. There were only five other people— a young couple, a nurse in scrubs and two waitresses in pink uniforms with aprons. The young ones were busy staring into each other's eyes, and the ladies didn't look like violent criminals. *Relax, but don't let down your guard.* She held up her window-side hand to cover her face in case Rafe happened to be outside peeking in. There was no sign of him.

She really didn't know what to think of the tall, handsome man who'd introduced himself as a pirate. On the plus side, he'd helped her escape from the bad guys. For that, she would be forever grateful. Then Rafe had taken off her clothes to treat her abrasions. *A plus or a minus?* Administering first aid counted as positive. Stripping an unconscious woman was…not good. She decided to leave the naked question aside. He'd taken her phone but left her wallet, which gave her enough cash to pay the buck-and-a-quarter fare for the streetcar. Rafe's really big negative, the one that counted, was obvious: he'd spent over two weeks spying on her. Still, if he climbed onto the streetcar right now and sat beside her, she wasn't sure whether she'd scream her head off or snuggle into his warm embrace.

If only life could be more black-and-white

with the good people wearing halos and devil horns for the bad ones. Some of the criminals she'd testified against were the very definition of evil. Monsters capable of committing terrible violence, they showed no remorse, possibly weren't capable of empathy. Rafe wasn't one of them, thank God. But could he work for them? Money spoke a universal language.

Hiring a private detective seemed too subtle for those thugs. She figured that if her enemies from Chicago found her, they'd take lethal revenge with a bullet in the gut or a knife across her throat or something more torturous and terrible. A shudder twitched across her shoulders. She couldn't trust WitSec, not anymore. Her survival depended on her ability to defend herself. During the last three years in New Orleans, she'd prepared a number of escape routes using new identities and different forms of transportation.

At her house, she had four sets of different license plates for her car, two prepacked suitcases, cash and the paperwork required to start over in another place. Unfortunately, going home was out of the question. The WitSec guy she'd recognized would know her address and would also know where she worked, which meant the emergency evacuation bag she'd hidden in the employees' locker room would have to be abandoned. Too bad! She had three disposable phones and a new credit identity in that bag.

Exiting at Canal Street, she blended into the smallish crowd on the street outside a restaurant. Closer to the French Quarter and the downtown area, there were more people—some in costume and some with masks. In her baggy T-shirt, she felt awkward, embarrassed and scared. The creeps in the skeleton masks had drugged her and nearly abducted her. What if they found her again? The fifteen minutes it took for the connecting streetcar seemed like hours. She climbed aboard, relieved when they finally jolted into motion.

Again, she shielded her face from those who could see her through the streetcar window. Peeking through her fingers, she stared out at the scraggly palm trees that lined Canal Street, barely looking up when a woman with long dreadlocks sat beside her.

"It's late," the woman said. "You hungry?"

"I am," Alyssa said, realizing as she spoke that the gnawing pain in her belly wasn't entirely due to injury. She needed to eat. "I'll stop at Café du Monde."

"The café got the finest beignets in the world." The woman chuckled, showing off three gold teeth. "You know what to do, how to take care of yourself. That's good. Rafe said you were a smart gal."

Rafe? Alyssa looked up sharply. Her gaze riveted on the woman sitting beside her who could have been anywhere from forty to 140. Strands of gray twined through her dreads, and her eye shadow was purple. She looked like she came from the voodoo shops in her long, dramatically patterned skirt, red and yellow tie-dyed tank top, and abundant jewelry.

"Excuse me," Alyssa said. "Did you say Rafe?"

"Such a pretty man, dontcha think? He tole me not to get you riled up, hon."

Alyssa was hit with a sense of déjà vu all over again. Meeting this woman felt a lot like when she danced with a pirate, caught a glimpse of her mom's ghost and woke up in a bedroom that looked like her own but wasn't. After the upside-down day she'd had, the approach of yet another odd person should have made her paranoid and scared, but her anger overwhelmed all other thoughts. No way would Alyssa play a cat-and-mouse game with this woman.

She wanted answers, and she wanted them now. "What's your name?"

"Everybody calls me Sheila Marie."

"Why did Rafe send you?"

"Wassamatter. You don't trust him?"

"Not a bit."

"Smart." Sheila Marie's eyebrows knitted, and her full lips pursed. "It's dangerous to put your trust in a man, any man. Rafe Fournier, the great-great-great-great-grandson of Pirate Jean-Pierre, is better than most. He's a good person but still a man. You know what I mean, hon? Can't help himself—his brain don't work right. And that's why he sent me."

"Let me get this straight," Alyssa said. "He thinks I'll trust you, a person I've never met, who has no credentials."

"Credentials," she said with another flash of gold teeth. "You think I should have a business card? Maybe a diploma?"

"I want to know what you do." Was she a psychic, a medium or a voodoo witch doctor with a dozen spells in her pocket? "If you had a business card, what would it say?"

"Mostly, I'm a helper. I'm good at finding people who have gone missing. The pirate said you were looking for a tall woman with silver curls."

Alyssa gasped. Her lungs clenched, and she stopped breathing. When Mom died, she'd tried to contact the spirit world and had thrown away hundreds of dollars on a fortuneteller in Chicago who came up empty. Did Sheila Marie have the answers? Could she make that connection? "Did you find her?"

"Not yet, it's only been a couple of hours." When she stood, her many necklaces and bangles jingled musically. "Come on now, this is our stop."

Café du Monde was right around the corner on St. Peter. "How did you find me?"

"Hush, hush. You'll find out soon enough."

Alyssa got off the trolley and walked arm in arm with her strange new companion to Café du Monde, a twenty-four-hour-a-day bakery that was always busy despite the fact that they didn't serve alcohol. She spotted Rafe standing at the far edge of the patio awning with a white bakery bag in his hand. In his brown leather jacket and blue jeans, he looked almost as dashing as when he'd been costumed as a pirate. Somehow, he seemed taller.

After he greeted Sheila with a kiss on each cheek and gave her the bag of beignets, he turned to Alyssa. "We need to be moving along, *cher.*"

She rooted her dancing shoes to the sidewalk, determined not to go any further without an explanation. "How did you know where to find me?"

"Secrets, secrets," Sheila Marie said with a snort. "You two deserve each other."

Rafe asked her, "Can you stick around for a while?"

"I'll do you one better, give you an escort. Follow me."

She entered the café, where she greeted several people like they were long-lost friends. When Rafe took Alyssa's arm to escort her, she resisted. This wasn't the escape she'd planned. She'd figured out every detail of how she could disappear, and she wouldn't let a stubborn pirate hold her back. "How did you know I was coming here?"

"Come with me, and I'll tell you."

Reluctantly, she followed in Sheila Marie's footsteps. "Start talking."

"Last week, when I was doing surveillance on you, I saw you come here. You bought beignets and drank a cup of chicory coffee. And then you walked a couple of blocks until you got to that old brick building halfway down the block with the painted advertisement for Zatarain's on the wall. You purposely walked past, then came back and went to the office where you paid cash for something to the guy at the front desk."

Why hadn't she noticed him? The whole reason she'd paused for coffee was to observe the area and make sure she wasn't being followed. "I must be blind."

"After you left, I checked with the office.

You're renting a storage space in that building. Don't worry, I didn't break into it." He tugged her forward. "Quit dragging your feet, *cher*. We need to hurry."

"Why?"

"As soon as you got in line for the Canal streetcar, I knew where you were headed. That's when I alerted Sheila Marie, who was close enough to intercept you. If I can figure out your escape plan, so can others."

Every word he said was logical. He was making sense, and she had to believe that her enemies could be here right now, watching and waiting. She might have ridden that cheerful red streetcar into a trap.

Chapter Five

Rafe's warning had the effect he wanted. He saw a glimmer of fear in her green eyes. Alyssa was still angry, no doubt about that, but she was also scared and she had good reason to be. If somebody was searching for her, they might have followed the same markers that led him to Canal Street.

Her gaze darted as she searched Café du Monde, trying to see the possible danger that might lurk among the mostly empty tables and twinkle lights. With the black Saints T-shirt hanging down to her knees and her hair a mass of tangles and the vestiges of ghost makeup on her face, she looked miserable and raggedy. Not like a person who belonged in this warm, fragrant bakery. Her voice creaked when she spoke. "Did you see anyone?"

"Not yet," he said.

"They could be anywhere," she whispered.

Sheila Marie handed Alyssa a cardboard cup

of chicory coffee, looked up at him and said, "You'd best find a place where Missy Alyssa can catch a few winks. This little birdie is ready to drop."

"Don't leave me," Alyssa pleaded with her. "You have to tell me about the silver-haired woman. She looked like my mom. And when she laughed, I heard my mom. I can't come so close and have her slip away."

"Hush now, honey." In a swoop, Sheila Marie gathered her into a one-arm embrace while holding her own coffee in her other hand. She spoke in warm, musical tones. "Your mama passed a few years back."

Rafe couldn't remember if he'd mentioned that detail to Sheila Marie, but he must have said something. Either that or his CI had hooked into her psychic abilities. Her voice was gentle but firm. "You listen to me, missy. Right now, you got to do like I tell you."

"But I—"

"Straighten up." She kissed Alyssa's forehead. "Come along now."

Sheila Marie shepherded them through the kitchen, where a minimal staff worked at a leisurely pace. A beignet is always better when eaten fresh; the bakers couldn't stockpile dozens in advance and had to keep cooking. The staff watched through droopy eyelids as Sheila

Marie escorted their little group through the kitchen and out a side door.

Rafe hadn't been able to make Alyssa budge, but Sheila Marie had everything under control. Contacting her was the smartest move he could have made. Instinctively, Alyssa seemed to trust the other woman. Never would she have allowed Rafe to take the lead. *Malchance*, it was bad luck for him. At times like this, he missed working for the FBI, where nobody questioned orders. They simply obeyed. Alyssa needed to accept his leadership. He couldn't be expected to choreograph a song-and-dance routine every time a decision had to be made.

Leaving the restaurant, they navigated through the streets until they came to a stop, huddled in a doorway. In a low murmur, he said, "Remember that you're in danger, *cher.*"

"I know."

"The men in masks tried to drag you off into the night."

"Yes," she said.

"You can't go jumping out the window of my safe house and running away. It's not safe."

"I don't trust you." In the reflected glow from a streetlamp, he watched her brow furrow as she continued, "This isn't your problem, Rafe. It's mine, and I can take care of myself. I have plans. I've made arrangements."

"Bless your heart," Sheila Marie said. "You got a former FBI agent who's over six feet tall and as pretty as he can be. Let him shoo away the bad guys."

Under his breath, Rafe said, "I'm not the only one who wants to protect her."

"Are you saying there's somebody bigger and badder than you?" Sheila Marie took a bite from her beignet, sending up a cloud of powdered sugar. "Do tell."

"WitSec." He focused on Alyssa. "Why haven't you called them?"

"I don't want to say."

"I'm not inclined to play guessing games."

"And I'm not going to tell you."

Stubborn, difficult woman! How had she survived until now? It wasn't easy to qualify for witness protection. Her refusal to take advantage of the well-run, efficient program must to be due to something more than orneriness. He glanced across the street. Halfway up the block was the tired old building he'd seen her enter. "Give me your key and tell me what you want me to take from your storage locker."

"I'll get it myself."

This was exactly the sort of situation he wanted to avoid. Rafe didn't want to waste time by listing the many reasons why she shouldn't act alone, starting with the obvious fact that she wasn't armed. If ambushed inside the storage building, she would need backup. A lookout on the street would be useful.

"Sheila Marie, I'd appreciate if you'd wait at the café and watch for suspicious characters." As if on cue, two zombie princesses walking a spotted Great Dane sashayed down the street. Half the city was suspicious-looking, but he trusted his CI to recognize real danger when she saw it.

When he reached down and took the gun from his ankle holster, Alyssa asked, "What's that?"

"A Glock 43 nine millimeter."

"I know it's a gun," she said. "I thought you were the type who carried a stun gun."

"I'm former FBI," he reminded her.

"Didn't you use a stun gun on the three skeletons?"

"I suit the weapon to the occasion. You're in serious trouble, *cher*." When he met her gaze, he silently repeated a mantra: *Don't come with me into the warehouse, don't come with me, don't come…* Aloud, he warned, "You should stay with Sheila Marie. Do as she says."

She shook her head, and her tangled curls bounced. "Compromise? I won't go in there alone. You can come with me. We need to go around to the back."

He waited for the headlights of a delivery van to pass before he stepped off the curb into the street with Alyssa close at his side. In spite of a slight limp, she moved athletically. From the first time he'd seen her, he'd known that she was healthy and fit. Part of her daily regimen always involved exercise. He'd enjoyed watching her workouts—a detail he would never share with her. She had already called him a stalker. He didn't want to graduate to pervert. A flagstone courtyard between the four-story Zatarain's building and the two-story neighbor to the left made it easy to access the loading dock at the rear. Up a short flight of concrete steps was a door. Before he could reach for the handle, Alyssa elbowed him out of the way.

"I've got this," she said.

On the back side of a metal post beside the door was a small box with a combination lock. With a few flicks of the wrist, she had it open. The key inside opened the door. Before entering, she slipped the key back into the box and closed it.

"You made arrangements," he said. "Smart."

"I figured I might need to get to my storage unit at odd hours. I pay extra every month for the lock combination."

He followed her into the warehouse. The silence hung heavily. The stink of dirt and rat droppings oozed from the brick walls. A faint glow from high windows thinned the darkness, but it was still hard to see anything but edges and shadows. He took a slim Maglite from his jacket pocket. The beam spotlighted a beat-up wooden desk, a couple of file cabinets and concrete floors that created a maze through the rows of boxes, lockers and storage units.

He didn't hear any other sounds and figured they were alone. Still, he didn't want to take chances. "Don't turn on the lights."

"You didn't happen to bring another flashlight, did you?"

"*Pardonnez-moi*, but no."

"How much can I take from storage?"

"Only as much as you can carry." He had to wonder what she'd packed into her unit. What items did she consider necessary to survival?

"You know," she said, "it would be easier if I had the flashlight. I'm the one who knows where we're going."

No argument. He handed over the Maglite. "I'm right behind you."

She set a vigorous pace, charging along a straight four-foot-wide path between wall lockers and smaller center units. At the end of the building, she made a sharp right. They stood in front of a freight elevator with an ancient wood-slat door that rolled up like a garage. She lifted it and stepped inside.

"C'mon," she said. "My locker is on the second floor."

He hated the idea of being trapped inside the rickety old elevator but didn't want to waste time arguing. Though the elevator was a wide area, designed to move large objects from one floor to the next, he felt tense and crowded. Under his lightweight leather jacket, he was sweating. When she pulled down the door and hit the button for the second floor, the machinery rumbled like ten swamp gators with indigestion.

"Too loud," he said, wishing he'd figured that logic earlier. "If anyone is here and planning an ambush, they know exactly where we are."

"You're right," she said. "I should have considered that."

As soon as the elevator door opened, he scooted out. Carelessly, he bumped her leg. When she winced and gasped, he jumped back and cursed himself for being so clumsy. Just a few hours ago, she'd been knocked around by those men in skeleton masks. Her bruises had had enough time to ripen.

"The pain," he asked, "is it bad?"

"I wouldn't mind a long soak in a hot bath."

Though her quest to escape infuriated him, he

had to admire her bravado. In spite of injuries and fear, her determination remained strong. She deserved every effort he could make to protect her.

The second floor of the warehouse was even more dreary and dark than the first. A few barred windows spilled light across rusted storage units. The big, square, filthy aluminum doors had numbers stenciled on the scarred, peeling paint. Her unit was 224.

She passed him the Maglite and reached under her giant T-shirt to retrieve her wallet and key chain. He focused the light so she could see where to unlock her unit.

"It's a five by five," she said. "I figured this was all the space I need."

The first thing he saw when she lifted the door was a sleek, shiny ten-speed bike that looked like it had never been ridden. She turned on the bare bulb light inside the unit, and he saw a tower of plain cardboard boxes pressed up against brand-new camping gear, still in the box. There was a tent, a sleeping bag, a camp stove, a lantern and miscellaneous tools, some with the price stickers still attached. Labels on other boxes showed premade food that was "better than the MRE."

He picked up a small hatchet. "Have you done much camping?"

"Not since I was a little girl and visited my grandparents in Georgia."

"How did you choose this equipment? Why?"

"I thought it might be a good idea to hide out in the backwoods. So I went to a sporting goods store and asked the salesman to give me all the gear I might need to survive for a month."

Rafe hoped the clerk had been working on commission. Providing the high-quality camping supplies this naive Yankee woman might need must have been an expensive proposition. "Did you happen to buy a gun?"

"Two of them," she said, "but I don't keep them here."

She climbed around the boxes and grabbed the heavy-duty straps on a gigantic backpack. As soon as she had access, she unzipped a small pocket on the side of the pack, dug inside and pulled out a bottle of extra-strength pain reliever. While she found a crate of bottled water in her space and helped herself, his cell phone buzzed, indicating he had a text message. Very few people had this number, which was specially encrypted so he couldn't be tracked or called unless he wanted to be.

He stepped away from her unit and checked his phone. The text came from Davidoff in Chicago. It was brief: Alyssa is missing. What do you know?

Rafe didn't reply. The message bothered him. Alyssa had been attacked by the three skeletons only a few hours ago. Already, Davidoff knew she'd gone off the grid. Where was he getting his information? Was somebody else keeping an eye on her? If others were involved, Davidoff should have informed him. Not that Rafe had expected ethical treatment from the infamous crime boss. Davidoff was no Boy Scout.

He glanced back toward the storage unit in time to see Alyssa strip off the oversize Saints T-shirt and change into a brown polo from her backpack. She'd already replaced her raggedy bloomers with a pair of jeans. Perched on the edge of a cardboard box, she changed into sneakers. With the addition of a denim jacket, her outfit was complete. Nondescript and practical, she'd blend in with any crowd. He couldn't explain why he preferred the zombie Scarlett clothes, but he did.

"Who was on the phone?" she asked.

"It was just a text." If she had been more forthcoming with him, he wouldn't have hesitated to share information.

"We should go," she said. "I have a hotel where you can drop me off."

Not a chance. She might think a local hotel was safe, but he doubted it. Rafe wouldn't abandon her to whatever thugs or skeletons might be on her trail. When they left this storage unit, he'd take her back to his safe house with the fully functional alarm system. On this issue, he refused to listen to any objection. Her safety was top priority. Either she came with him or she went to WitSec.

She hefted the backpack, which was almost as big as she was, onto her shoulders, grabbed the Maglite and staggered to the end of the row, where a casement window allowed a square of moonlight to spill across the concrete floor. This window started at her waist and went vertical for four feet. In summer, it could be cranked open and used for ventilation.

Alyssa peered through the grungy panes of glass. "Oh, no."

"Qu'est-ce que c'est?" He moved down the aisle toward her. "What's wrong?"

She pointed to the window. "There's a man across the street. I recognize him."

He peered through the window. The silhouette of a man—average height and weight—was readily visible. Though dressed in black, this guy wasn't good at fading into the shadows. He stood just outside the alley with the streetlamp illuminating his features. "How do you know him?"

"He's the man behind the skeleton mask that I pulled off. I realized that I'd seen him before, but it wasn't until just now that I recalled his name."

"Who is he?"

"Hugh Woodbridge," she said.

His phone buzzed again. He glanced down at a text from Sheila Marie that said, Three bad guys incoming. Get out!

Across the street, he saw two others join Woodbridge. "Why do you know this man?"

Her voice was a strangled whisper. "I saw him in the offices at WitSec."

That explained why she couldn't call witness protection for assistance. She'd been betrayed. "Woodbridge is a US marshal."

"I'm afraid so."

Bad news for her...for both of them.

Chapter Six

Alyssa watched Woodbridge and his two colleagues saunter across the street toward the warehouse. They were coming after her again. She'd been running on adrenaline ever since she regained consciousness, and her energy was almost depleted. Her backpack felt like it weighed a thousand pounds. Her vision was foggy. Her bruises ached. Escape from this warehouse without Rafe's help would be nearly impossible. At this point, she had to trust him, even though he was an admitted pirate/ex–federal agent/private eye who'd been hired by an unnamed shady character to spy on her.

She tilted her head to look up at him. "Do you have a plan?"

He took the Maglite from her hand and replaced it with his Glock 43. "Don't shoot unless I tell you."

No need to worry about that. She'd never

fired a gun at a living being and doubted she'd be able to start now. "Is the safety on?"

"Don't touch the trigger, and you'll be fine."

She followed him back to her storage space, where he used the flashlight to dig through her belongings until he found what he was looking for—a generous length of woven blue rope and a couple of those metal clippy things. He pulled down the door to her unit, closed it and locked it. "You ought to send a thank-you note to the sales clerk who ordered your gear. I doubt you asked for rock-climbing equipment."

"Rock climbing?"

"The rope and carabiners," he said. "These supplies might save us."

Before she could open her mouth to ask questions, she heard loud noises from downstairs. *A door being flung open? The heavy tread of men in boots?* They'd broken into the building.

Now was the time for action. And Rafe didn't hesitate. He seemed comfortable giving orders, which, she supposed, was SOP for FBI agents or captains of pirate ships. Whichever identity suited him was fine with her. Too nervous to think or plan, she fell into line, ready to do whatever he said.

He stopped in front of a casement window, which he managed to crank open. A breeze swept into the warehouse. Only a few blocks from the river, the air felt damp.

"Take off your backpack," he said.

"Will I have to leave it behind? There are things in there that I need."

"We'll take it, but you can't carry that much weight."

As soon as she slipped the straps off her shoulders, she felt better—not much stronger but lighter. She watched him use the carabiners to secure the woven blue rope around a pillar beside the window. After it was fastened, he tied a knot near the end.

"What are you doing?" she asked.

"Making a loop. Stick your toe into the loop, and I'll lower you down."

"That's a long drop. I could break my leg."

"Which is why I will lower you," he said. "Let me help you climb onto the sill."

The window opening was wide enough for her to pass through. From downstairs, she heard the rumbling squawk of the freight elevator as it descended to the first floor. Woodbridge was coming closer. She stuck her foot into the loop. "Now what?"

"Put your weight on your foot in the loop and slip through the window. Hold tight to the rope, and I'll let you down gradually. Brace yourself against the side of the warehouse."

Peering down, she stared at the narrow side-walk between buildings. The drop was only about thirty feet but seemed as deep as an abyss. This window was strategically placed on the only side of the building that wasn't exposed to public view. The loading dock was in the rear. The front opened onto the street. And the opposite side looked down on the flagstone court-yard.

Though she tried to prepare herself for the descent, her hands trembled. Her bruises throbbed. She was so weak! How the hell was she going to jump out a window and climb down the side of a building like a spider?

"I can't do it," she said. "Do you have a plan B?"

"We're out of time."

Woodbridge and his men were calling to each other as they made their way through the storage units. Rafe was right, again. There wasn't a spare moment for hesitation or logic or fear. She climbed through the window, used the loop to support her weight and held the blue woven rope with all the strength she could muster. Slowly, he lowered her. Her leg began to buckle, and she kicked against the wall.

Above her, Rafe offered encouragement. "You're almost there."

She looked down. Not that far from the

ground, she hesitated while he lowered her another few feet, and then she swung her free leg
until her foot touched the sidewalk. She'd made
it.

Gasping, she collapsed on the ground, unfastened the toe loop and watched as the blue
rope snaked up the side of the building toward
Rafe. He leaned out the window and dropped
her backpack. Quickly, he climbed into the window frame.

She noticed that he was wearing black gloves
as he held the woven rope. He braced his feet
against the wall and climbed down. His descent
looked easy, almost graceful.

"We made it," he said.

"We did."

For the first time, she thought of them as a
unit. They were no longer him and her—their
escape had turned *them* into *we*. He had saved
her and protected her. Was he, finally, the one
person in the whole world she could trust?

He hoisted her backpack to his shoulders.
"Come."

From the window above, she heard voices.
Looking up, she didn't see anyone peeking out,
but Woodbridge and his men were on the move,
coming closer. She had no time for questions
or planning. No time to handle the situation
in the organized manner she preferred. All she

could do was run down the alley behind Rafe. Usually, she was fast and agile. She prided herself on staying in shape with workouts, sprints and three-mile runs twice a week. But now, she stumbled on every other step. *Exhausted. Clumsy.*

When they got to the street, two blocks down from Café du Monde, Rafe grasped her arm and rushed her along the sidewalk. He stopped beside a motorcycle, took a helmet from the luggage carrier and handed it to her. "Put it on."

Not her favorite form of transportation, but she wouldn't argue. They had to get away fast; these streets were too vulnerable. He fastened her backpack onto a rear luggage rack and helped her climb onto his bike. Before he got on, he flipped up the visor on her helmet, stared into her eyes and asked, "Are you strong enough to hold on?"

"I can make it." Though she'd agreed to let him take the lead, she didn't want him to think she was a wimp. "There's no other choice. Turning myself over to the cops is no guarantee of safety, not with a US marshal on my tail."

"About Woodbridge," he said. "No more secrets."

"The same goes for you."

"A question, *cher*." He stroked his jawline and

massaged the dimple in his chin. "May I ask why these guys are really after you?"

"It's got to be revenge," she said. "My testimony got one guy a life sentence and prison terms for three others."

He leaned closer. His gray eyes were mesmerizing. "Tell me why a US marshal in New Orleans would care about the prison term for thugs from Chicago."

Breaking eye contact with him, she glanced over her shoulder. "We should get moving."

"If they want you dead, why not hire a sniper to shoot you on the street?"

"They don't want my death to be easy. They want to hurt me. That's the only thing that makes sense."

She refused to think about the other possibilities and unknown dangers that had haunted her ever since the FBI came knocking on her door asking for her testimony. Her old boss, Max Horowitz, had been a fence who owned a pawnshop. While working for him, she'd entered millions of dollars—receipts and billing, payments and expenses—into her neat ledgers. She was aware that a certain level of danger was attached to handling that much money. The FBI asked a million questions about the balances.

"It's possible," Rafe said, "that you have something they want."

"Not your problem." The moment of trust had passed. She returned to her normal, suspicious attitude. "If you don't mind, I'd like to be dropped off at a hotel. The address is—"

"I'm still in charge, *cher*. You go where I tell you." He put on his helmet and mounted the bike. "Hang on."

Alyssa wrapped her arms around his torso. His body was lean and muscular, radiating with heat. That warmth comforted her, even though he was being deliberately contentious. He cranked the bike, and the engine roared to life, sending shivers through her body. She tightened her hold and leaned against his broad back, rubbing her cheek against the supple leather of his jacket.

Though perfectly capable of taking care of herself, she had to admit that she liked being with Rafe. What had Sheila Marie called him? A former fed who was tall and dark and pretty. He was protecting her, and that level of concern felt unfamiliar to her. Mom had done her best to take care of Alyssa, but Mom was flighty—more attuned to playing games and having fun than providing a safe environment for her daughter. Alyssa's aunt Charlotte had never been someone she could turn to for wisdom or help. Mr. Horowitz was kind, but he was only her employer. There had never really been anyone who was dedicated to defending Alyssa. Not when she was growing up and certainly not now.

As the motorcycle swerved around a street corner, she leaned into the turn. The breeze wove around them, and she was glad to be wearing her denim jacket and jeans. Before she could get her bearings and figure out which street they were on, Rafe yanked the handlebars to the right and drove the bike into an alley. Where was he taking her? When they emerged from the alley, she heard jazzy music and laughter from a bar on the corner. The sign above the bar identified it as Hurricane Harry's, named after a signature rum drink with a cherry and orange slice garnish. A woman dancing on the sidewalk looked like Sheila Marie…or maybe not.

Her memories blurred with glimpses of street scenes. When Rafe drove on the long, open stretch at the river's edge, she gave up trying to determine their destination and closed her eyes. Images from the parade flashed through her mind. She remembered the skeletons. Why did they come after her? Rafe's question had been perceptive. If they wanted her dead, why not just shoot her?

After dozens more twists and turns, he exited the street and drove up a driveway. She opened her eyes as he parked on the breezeway beside the house—the same house she'd escaped from only a few hours ago. "We're back here?"

He climbed off the bike and removed his helmet. "I told you I used to work for the FBI. You remember?"

She nodded.

"I know how to set up a safe house. You need surveillance, weapons and secrecy. Done, done and done. I have cameras, sound and motion detectors, infrared vision—all the bells and whistles. There's plenty of weapons, the more high-tech the better. And nobody knows this hideout exists. You're more protected here than in a hotel."

"What about your client? He must know the address."

"Let me worry about him."

When she dismounted from the motorcycle, her legs were rubbery. Too exhausted to think, she'd ask other questions in the morning. Right now, all she wanted was sleep.

AFTER RAFE GOT her settled in bed and activated the security systems that turned this plain little house into a digital fortress, he sat at the kitchen table and took out his cell phone. He'd told Alyssa that he could take care of his client, and it was time to make good on that promise. The conversation would be difficult. Rafe had been hired by Davidoff to protect Alyssa, which didn't mean that the Chicago gangster had good intentions. By reputation, he was smooth but ruthless—much more dangerous than a rogue federal marshal like Woodbridge. Why was Davidoff so interested in this young woman?

Davidoff had fired off four more text messages, each more demanding that the one that came before. He went from the first polite inquiry about Alyssa's whereabouts to a demand. The last one, received at 3:17 in the morning, said, Where R U? Call me. Now.

Another benefit of Rafe's safe house security was a cybershield that made it impossible to trace his computers and cell phones. It was now 3:34. Rafe put through his call on the phone number Davidoff had given him. Audio only—he didn't want to show a glimpse of the house.

"Why, why, why…" Davidoff spat the words, rapid-fire like a semiautomatic. "Why did you take so long to call back?"

"Prior engagement."

"A woman? Is that it? Did you ignore my text because you're getting laid?"

"I have been with a woman this evening," Rafe said truthfully. "But tonight was about the celebration of *Día de los Muertos*, Day of the Dead. I had hoped to contact my pirate ancestors."

"Your voodoo games and your sex life don't interest me. Tell me about Alyssa."

Though Rafe had never actually met Viktor Davidoff, aka Davis James, aka Diamond Jim the owner of six used-car lots in Chicago, he'd done plenty of research before accepting this job. Photos showed Davidoff to be heavyset with shoulders like a bull and a thick neck. His head was shaved, and his black beard was neatly trimmed into a goatee. Though he had a reputation for being well dressed, Davidoff had the strong hands of a peasant, with thick, blunt fingers.

If Rafe expected to learn anything from this client, he needed to ask the right questions and avoid giving away too much. "When do you think Alyssa went missing?"

"After her shift at the restaurant, she didn't return to her house."

"She might have a date."

Davidoff scoffed. "You've been watching her. Does she have a boyfriend?"

"Tonight, there are parties in the street. She could have arranged a casual meeting." Rafe shifted the direction of the conversation back toward the other man. "Do you have someone watching her house? Who told you she wasn't at home?"

"Should have been you!" Davidoff fired his

accusation like a bullet. "I'm paying you good money to watch over the girl. And don't get me started on your so-called expenses."

Setting up the bedroom to his client's specifications had been costly, but Rafe turned the focus back on Davidoff. "Have you hired someone else to handle your business in New Orleans?"

"Why the hell would I do that? I'm not made of money."

"Who told you Alyssa was missing?"

"Not that it's any of your business, but it was the FBI agent who recommended that I hire you as a bodyguard."

"That was Jessop, yes?"

"I never said his name."

"But I'm correct." As soon as Davidoff had contacted him, Rafe had his FBI computer whiz do a search, and he'd found a link. "Your contact in the FBI is Darren Jessop, *n'est-ce pas*?"

"I don't have to tell you a damn thing, Frenchie. You work for me, got it?"

"But of course."

"I want to know where the hell she is."

Rafe decided to let this fish off the hook. "She's spending the night in a safe location. I can guarantee that she won't be harmed. Tomorrow at noon, I'll send you a photo of her."

"Thank God."

His relief sounded genuine. "She's important to you. Why?"

"Let's just say that I knew her mom well."

Davidoff didn't seem like the kind of man who took a sentimental journey. There had to be another reason for him to be invested in Alyssa's safety, and it probably involved money. Rafe probed, "In her job for the pawnbroker, she handled money. Is there some sort of payoff?"

"I'm done talking, Frenchie. Send me her picture tomorrow." He paused. "Maybe it's time for me to come to New Orleans myself. Alyssa will be happy to see me."

Rafe had his doubts. "Does she even know you?"

"We've met." He gave a sinister chuckle. "You might say I'm the most important man in her life."

"Why is that?"

"Let's just say that without me, she would never have been born."

Davidoff was her father?

Chapter Seven

The next morning, Rafe woke up thinking about the Chicago gangster with the thick neck and stubby fingers. If Davidoff truly was Alyssa's papa, he had a good, even noble, reason to hire a bodyguard to watch over her. But his claim was hard to believe. According to Rafe's internet search, no father was listed on her birth certificate. No man had claimed to be her parent, not in Chicago or in Savannah, where she'd lived with her mama for a few years.

Last night before she fell asleep, Alyssa had spoken about her family. She'd told him that her papa stepped out of her life when she was five years old. She never knew his name. Her mama said he was dead, and she had no reason to think otherwise.

Sitting on the edge of his bed, Rafe stretched and yawned. The early light of dawn crept through the window blinds. It was only a few minutes past seven, which was early for him and most of the NOLA night owls, but three and a half hours of sleep would have to be enough. He knew Alyssa was an early riser.

If Davidoff was her papa, why hadn't he come forward before now? After her mama died, Alyssa had no other family. When she'd witnessed a murder, she'd almost been killed before she was taken into protective custody. What kind of father would abandon his daughter when she so desperately needed him? Diamond Jim was a powerful, dangerous man who wielded great influence. Maybe he thought he was doing Alyssa a favor by distancing himself. If his enemies didn't know of her existence, they wouldn't go after her.

If those were the true circumstances, Davidoff could be considered gallant. But Rafe didn't think that was so. More likely, Davidoff was after the so-called payoff—a mysterious stash gleaned from the accounts of Alyssa's boss. When Special Agent Jessop referred Davidoff to Rafe, he'd mentioned that Alyssa was not only pretty but might have access to serious money. Rafe should question Jessop and dig out more information, but he had reservations about contacting the feds. Yesterday, Jessop had reported to Davidoff that Alyssa was missing. Had he also betrayed her WitSec location? *Très suspicious, n'est-ce pas*? Agent Jessop could be hooked up with the US Marshals. It might be wiser to keep the FBI in the dark.

Without turning on the light, he got out of bed. If he'd been alone, he wouldn't have bothered with clothes. But Alyssa was here. He pulled on a pair of sweatpants and shuffled barefoot into the kitchen. First order of business: brewing a pot of chicory-flavored coffee.

After he set the coffee to perk, he checked his surveillance cameras and alarm systems. All clear. He hustled down the hallway to the single bathroom in the house. The door was locked. From inside, he heard water running. Alyssa had gotten there first, which shouldn't be a problem. He knew from observing her that she typically hopped into and out of the shower in less than fifteen minutes, even when she washed her hair.

Back in the kitchen, he poured himself a mug of coffee. His brain would work better after a hit of caffeine—maybe then he could figure out who was after her and why. This morning, Alyssa ought to be more willing to share information. Hadn't he saved her cute little buns last night? Surely her opinion of him had changed.

Last night at the storage facility, there had been a moment when she let down her guard and trusted him. He needed that attitude to continue. Acting as her bodyguard was hard enough without having to worry about her sneaking out windows and taking off on some improbable scheme. He considered his plans for the day. If she agreed to cooperate, he could leave her safely tucked away in this house, where the security was top-notch. But he couldn't be one hundred percent sure that no one could track her to this location. If the bad guys found her, she didn't have the skills to defend herself. Therefore, he had to bring her with him when he left the house.

He sipped his coffee. Today he should consult with Chance—the computer genius—in order to uncover information on Davidoff and on Alyssa's former boss, the Chicago pawnbroker. And, of course, he'd talk to Sheila Marie to find out the gossip on the street. First, he needed to get into the bathroom.

Peeking down the hallway of this narrow, shotgun-style house, he saw her walking toward him, wrapped in a blue, yellow and orange beach towel. Her hair was still damp from the shower. The overhead light in the hallway spread a golden mantle across her bare shoulders. Her cheeks flushed pink. Her eyes were bright. "Good morning, Rafe."

"Allo, cher."

Her gaze dropped to his naked chest. "I didn't expect to see quite so much of you."

His nascent plan to assert his authority disappeared. With nothing more than a smile, she had disarmed him. "I made coffee," he said.

"I'll throw on clothes and join you in the kitchen." She tossed her head. "We need to make plans. Because it's Sunday, I can't get into the safe-deposit box at my bank. But I have other things to do before I leave town."

"It is not safe for you to leave New Orleans before you have a safe destination and a plan."

"It's worse if I stay," she said. "And I'm good at figuring out what to do. I'll need to use your computer to look for locations."

Instead of objecting, he dived into the bathroom. The mirror was still steamed over from her shower, and he could only see a hazy outline of himself, which was fine with him. Rafe didn't want to confront himself directly after allowing Alyssa to roll over him. The way she talked about her plans sounded like she was calling the shots.

He rushed through a shower, brushed his teeth and dressed in cargo pants and a T-shirt. Though he was moving fast, she beat him back to the kitchen. When he entered, she was on tiptoe, reaching for a high shelf in the cabinet. Her mint-green blouse rode up, giving him a glimpse of her silky midriff.

"I thought I'd make oatmeal," she said. "Why do you keep it way up here?"

"I prefer grits," he said. "Step aside, I'll cook breakfast."

He took the container of stone-ground grits from the lower shelf and got started while she settled herself at the square-topped wooden table.

She tasted her coffee. "If there's anything I can do to help, just tell me."

Without measuring, he poured milk and water into a saucepan to heat. Grits for breakfast had been a standard since childhood, when Grandmama Lucille prepared most of the meals for his active family. Both his parents were professors at Tulane, and his three sisters were older and busy with their own lives. Nana Lucille had taught him how to cook, and he'd enjoyed his time in the kitchen where the air was redolent with Cajun spices and his mouth watered in anticipation of the treats to come. The kitchen was a soothing place, good for talking.

"I know the basics of how you came to be in WitSec," he said, "but it would be useful to hear the details from you."

She groaned. "I've told this story a gazillion times. Are you sure you need to hear it?"

"We need to determine who is after you and why. So, yes, *s'il vous plaît*, tell me how you got yourself into so much trouble. Start with your old boss."

"Max Horowitz?"

"How did a nice girl like you get a job working for someone like him?"

"Through my mom," she said. "Mr. Horowitz used to come into the jewelry store where Mom worked as an appraiser. Long story short, she arranged for me to take a part-time job at his pawnshop after school, which was a huge step up from the pizza joint where I'd been working."

He set the cast-iron skillet on the range to heat before he cooked the bacon. The part of her account that she'd omitted with a casual "long story short" intrigued him. "What else was going on in your life at that time?"

"It was about ten years ago, just after Aunt Charlotte ran off and was killed in a fire. Mom missed her and spent a lot of time crying. She wasn't purposely ignoring me, but I felt isolated. I liked the distraction of working."

He glanced at her over his shoulder, noticing that she'd used the coffee mug with daisies that he seldom touched. "Did your mama know that Horowitz was a fence?"

"Are you insinuating that my mom didn't take good care of me?"

"You tell me, *cher.*"

"When she was in a good mood, she was the

best—beautiful, funny and talented. On weekends, she used to sing with a band at weddings and, of course, with the choir at church." Alyssa fluffed her still-damp curls. "Mom raised me by herself. Money was tight. Not that we were broke or anything. But there were times when she might have dabbled in petty crime—things we didn't talk about. She never hurt anybody, always had my best interests at heart."

Her tone had become defensive and sharp. She loved her mama and wouldn't tolerate any negative allegations against her, even if they were true. He had to wonder about her mom's untimely death, killed in a hit-and-run.

"And so," he said, "you took a nice, quiet office job as an accountant in a pawnshop."

"I jumped on it. Mr. Horowitz was a sweet older gentleman."

According to internet gossip, that kindly old man with his walrus mustache and rumpled suit had stabbed a robber with a sword disguised as an umbrella. "Tell me about your job."

"The office was on the second floor of the pawnshop on the Near West Side, which was a fairly decent neighborhood. Mr. Horowitz assured my mom that it wasn't dangerous, and he did everything he could to make sure that was true. When I got to work, he buzzed me in. The door between the staircase leading up to my office and the shop was always locked. There were only four attempted burglaries during the five years I worked there."

"Only?" He stirred the grits and turned the bacon in the skillet.

"Pawnshops are tempting targets for thieves. It's a cash business. Mr. Horowitz had a built-in safe in addition to the cash register." She left the table and joined him at the stovetop. "I'll do the grits. You take the bacon."

He'd considered frying up andouille sausage to mix with the grits but decided to keep it simple. Making an incredible breakfast wasn't his primary goal. He wanted her to relax and give him the real story. But he didn't want her to make a mess with his food. "Have you made grits before?"

"I'm a cook at a bistro."

He'd wondered why she'd taken that job. When her mom died, Alyssa had been left with substantial assets and a big insurance payoff. She didn't need the money. "Do you enjoy being a chef?"

"Not as much as I thought I would. All the food in New Orleans sounds so exotic—gumbo, jambalaya, crawfish étouffée. Learning how to make those dishes isn't easy, and I've had several disasters."

He liked her curiosity and her interest in his

hometown. So much about her was appealing. "You mentioned burglaries," he said. "Did you get involved in one of them? Is that how you ended up in witness protection?"

"You are so wrong. The incident didn't come until later, and it didn't happen at the pawnshop." Using a wooden spoon, she swirled the grits. "Should I add butter?"

"If you like."

"Everything is sweeter with butter."

"Spoken like a true daughter of the South."

"Don't forget," she said, "when you first met me, I was dressed as Scarlett O'Hara. I'm not a belle, but my mom was born and bred in Savannah. I've spent enough time there to understand their customs and habits. Not to mention the past few years I've lived in New Orleans. I like this town, and I'll be sad to leave."

"Perhaps, *cher*, we can find a way for you to stay."

She shook her head. "The best thing is to pack up my tent and move far away. In a new city, I can start over."

"And if they find you again?"

"I'll stay on the move."

While leaning over her shoulder to check the grits, he caught a whiff of her hair, a peach fragrance that didn't smell like any shampoo he'd ever bought. She must have brought her own hair products in that giant backpack. When he inhaled again, she turned her head. Their faces were inches apart. The tip of her nose almost touched his chin.

Kissing her lips would have been natural, sexy, pleasant and…*très, très, très stupide*. Such intimacy was destined to end in a slap. He pulled back and said, "Cayenne. I like to add pepper to the grits."

"So do I." She stirred in salt, a pinch of cayenne and a glob of butter. "I like my food sweet and spicy."

Precisely the way he liked his women. Not a topic he intended to mention to her, not even as a joke. "Tell me more about your work at the pawnshop."

"Mr. Horowitz made it easy for me. At various times during the day, he handed over paperwork that showed what merchandise had been taken in and how much he paid for it. I recorded the transaction in a digital file that could be checked against the counter receipts. After I'd been there for a couple of months, I started doing larger shipments that were delivered to the warehouse. After that, I recorded estate sales where Mr. Horowitz picked up antiques and artwork. Sometimes, Mom went along on those trips."

Her work sounded straightforward. Products

came in and cash went out. "I suppose the business expenses had their own records."

"There were several different files. Mr. Horowitz liked to see monthly figures, detailed quarterly tax data, profit and loss statements to verify how much he was spending on different parts of the business. Everything was computerized, but my boss was old-fashioned. He liked the ledger system that he'd used when he first went into business."

"How did you do that?"

"I translated the figures by hand from the computer to neat, tidy books. Some were bound in leather. Others were less fancy. He kept them on floor-to-ceiling shelves behind his antique desk in the upstairs office. My workstation was across the room by the window."

Rafe took the skillet filled with thick strips of bacon off the flame. "Are you saying that there were two sets of books?"

"Actually, there were three. I used to take a photo with my phone of the computer sheets to copy into the other ledger. Before you get all excited, I should tell you that FBI forensic accountants went over the ledgers and other data. They were satisfied that Mr. Horowitz wasn't committing fraud."

Still, the complicated system was suspicious and offered many opportunities for disguising amounts and burying payments. Using a high school part-timer to keep track of business accounting seemed risky. While she finished with the grits and sprinkled cheddar on top, he whipped up scrambled eggs. With breakfast assembled, he sat across the table from her and raised his coffee mug in a toast.

"Here's to us," she said.

"And here's to finding the men who are after you…"

"…and locking them up in handcuffs, and then we'll throw them into a swamp, where the gators eat them piece by bloody piece."

Her grin belied the danger in her words. Not unlike the zombie Scarlett she impersonated, Alyssa had many secrets she hadn't revealed. For one thing, she made the pawnshop sound like a cute little neighborhood business. He knew better. Horowitz Pawn & Exchange had been a multimillion-dollar business. Not only did the old man with the white mustache deal in over-the-counter trades, but he handled raw diamonds and antique jewelry with untraceable provenance. And he was a fence who regularly dealt with criminals and probably laundered their cash.

Though the FBI accountants hadn't found evidence of fraud, that didn't mean her boss had been cleared. When Alyssa came forward to testify, Max Horowitz had disappeared. He hadn't been heard from since.

"We should make plans," she said. "I'd love to get into my house."

"A joke?" Because he wasn't laughing.

"I realize that it would be difficult, but I hate to lose everything I own."

She might be hiding something of significance at the house. "Any particular item? Perhaps jewelry?"

"As if I'd be foolish enough to leave anything valuable lying around."

"*Mais non*, you are too clever." He watched her expression as he continued. "You might have hidden something under a loose floorboard or in a secret compartment of a desk or in the freezer section of your refrigerator."

"I might have tried a stunt like that...when I was twelve." While holding eye contact and looking innocent, she dug into her breakfast and moaned with pleasure at the first taste of grits. "If Mr. Horowitz taught me anything, it was how to keep my treasures safe. My mom was the same way. When I was a kid, we used to play a game where she'd hide a diamond brooch and I had to find it."

"And now that you're grown up?"

"Well, you saw my storage unit. And I mentioned my safe deposit boxes. I have a locker in a gym and at my work."

Her green eyes sparkled so brightly that he was distracted. He looked forward to the time when she stopped playing this game of cat-and-mouse with him. They were on the same side. The more he knew, the better he could protect her. "In any case, you cannot return to your house. They could be watching or have rigged booby traps. Your car will most certainly have a tracking system so they can find you."

"You might be interested to know that I have another car. It's in a private garage, all gassed up and ready to roll."

"Is this vehicle in your name?"

She bit off a piece of bacon with her sharp, white teeth and chewed before washing it down with coffee. "Technically, Alyssa Bailey is an alias. That's the name I use for everyday business, but I have four other identities, two with passports and all with credit cards."

It sounded like she changed names the way other people changed clothes. "Did you have any of this paperwork while you lived in Chicago?"

"Only one," she said. "I added the others during my three years in New Orleans."

She made falsifying her identity sound like a hobby. Where had she gotten the paperwork?

How had she obtained credit in different names? He suspected that Horowitz had taught her more than rudimentary accounting procedures. "I would like to see these documents."

"Not a good idea. After all, I might need to disappear from you." She dabbed at her full lips with a paper napkin. "Maybe we can pick up my second car or visit the locker at my health club."

"We'll see."

He had no intention of allowing her to call the shots and drag him along on her secret and possibly nefarious agenda. After another sip of coffee, he scooped up a forkful of fluffy scrambled eggs. The food was good, but he ate too fast and only savored every other bite. Alyssa had thrown him off his game.

After they cleaned up the breakfast dishes, he took her into the small pantry off the kitchen so he could show her his array of surveillance equipment. Four screens from cameras outside the house were divided into four smaller pictures. None showed suspicious activity.

He explained the sensors. "If you jiggle the doorknobs or rattle the windows, an alert rings through on my cell phone."

"Last night, you knew exactly when I made my escape." Her tone became accusatory. "Why didn't you stop me?"

"I wanted to see where you'd go."

"And why is that, Rafe? Did you think I'd be meeting a contact?" She whirled to confront him. The walls of this tiny room seemed to shrink as she demanded, "Do you suspect me?"

That was a big question with many shades of gray between gleaming innocence and pitch-black guilt. Hoping not to destroy the cooperative mood that had been building during breakfast, he distracted her by holding up her cell phone and replacing the battery. "If you want to check messages, you can turn it on for a few minutes. I have enough security in this house to shield phone transmission and tracking."

She snatched the phone. "Thank you."

He watched her scroll through texts and messages. Her manner was casual, and he didn't sense that she was looking for a contact from a partner in crime. "Are you expecting a call?"

She shrugged. "I have a message here from Anonymous. Should I play it?"

He perched on a stool in front of the screens. "If you please…"

The voice of Anonymous reminded him of her earlier account. Pitched low with husky overtones, Anonymous could have been male or female. The message was brief: "Sunday morning, nine o'clock services at the Hope and Peace Church in the Ninth Ward. Be there."

She played it again. "That's the same person who called me last night. I'm sure of it."

"But you don't recognize the voice."

"There's something familiar, but no."

He glared at the phone in her hand. Though he wasn't in the mood to dash across town without knowing what he was looking for, they couldn't ignore this message. "You need to get dressed in a hurry. We're going to church."

She bounced to her feet. "Give me eight minutes."

Most women would take longer than that to put on makeup and style their hair, but Alyssa was a clever little chameleon. In his bedroom, Rafe changed into a dark blue suit and a white shirt with no tie. Before he donned the jacket, he added a shoulder holster. Then he ran a finger over his jaw. No time to shave, but he wasn't too scruffy-looking. He combed through his thick, dark hair with his fingers and called out, "Ready?"

"Almost."

He stepped into the hallway and came face-to-face with a blonde whose long hair curled past her shoulders. Out of curiosity, he checked his watch. Exactly eight minutes had passed. "How did you know the timing?"

"I've practiced changing into my disguise." She wore extra-large black sunglasses with rhinestones in the corners. Her patterned pink sundress had a full skirt and low-cut neckline. With her fists on her hips, she stuck out her impressive cleavage. Then she pursed her lips, which were painted neon pink, and asked, "What do you think, sugar?"

"Subtle."

Alyssa Bailey, the former accountant from Chicago, had transformed into a femme fatale. Those huge sunglasses hid her green eyes. The bright color of her dress was a distraction. Any witness describing her would focus on the long shiny blond hair. She had a natural talent for disappearing in plain sight. Rafe had years of undercover experience, and he approved of her disguise.

Chapter Eight

In moments, they were out the door and on their way, riding in the black SUV that had been parked in the detached garage behind the house. Scrunched down in the passenger seat, Alyssa felt twitchy and nervous. Not scared—not yet, anyway. The misty morning sunlight spread a sultry glow over the city streets near the French Quarter. Last night's parade had left behind debris. Mingled with the trash and discarded flowers were glittery threads of fine memories. New Orleans was like a woman who'd spent the night in the throes of passion and was well pleased with herself on the morning after.

Alyssa envied the sensual indolence of NOLA. In comparison, she seldom allowed herself to relax, seldom let her guard down. When her life whirled off balance, she hated the disorientation from scary memories in the past and the threats of the future.

Behind her giant sunglasses, her brow furrowed. She had to remember and to plan and, above all, to trust no one—not even Rafe, even though he seemed to be helping her. In his blue suit and crisp white shirt, he looked as sharp and well groomed as any other gentleman on a Sunday morning. But not harmless. His eyes flicked from left to right and back again, scanning for danger as he drove. She hadn't missed the fact that he wore a shoulder holster under his jacket.

With the sun visor pulled down, she took off her glasses and studied her reflection in the mirror. *More blush, more lipstick.* When she first started playing with makeup, she'd been amazed by how simple it was to change her appearance with a wig, eyeliner and a push-up bra. The bra had proved especially effective. Most men— and some women—were so impressed with her bosom that they barely noticed her face.

When she unpacked last night, she'd had a feeling that a disguise might be necessary and had taken this pink outfit that she'd named Baby Doll from her backpack. She'd shaken out the long blond curls and hung up the dress. Though she would have preferred platform heels to complete Baby Doll, her backpack was only big enough for pink ballet flats, which was probably just as well. She wanted to be appropriate for church.

Glancing over at Rafe, she asked, "Am I dressed okay?"

"You look fine."

That rote response was the kind of thing men said to stay out of arguments. It didn't tell her much. "Where I grew up in Savannah, our church was nondenominational Christian with a super-dramatic pastor, a lot of clapping and singing. Mom was a soloist in the choir, and she was really good. When she sang 'Ave Maria,' the congregation wept."

"Are you sure you're her child?" He teased, "I ask because I heard your singing voice at the parade. You almost made me cry, but not in a good way."

"I didn't inherit her talent." And she didn't appreciate the reminder. "Is the Hope and Peace Church the kind of place I'll feel comfortable in a wig and sunglasses?"

"Don't know, *cher*. I've never been there."

The location and the anonymous phone call worried her. "Why do you suppose the mystery caller wants to meet at a church?"

He shrugged. "The message was left on your phone. And so, I suspect, the location is meant to have some kind of significance for you. When you think of church, what comes to mind?"

She closed her eyelids and concentrated. She hadn't been a regular churchgoer in years, and her memories were mostly of Bible stories and games they played in Sunday school. "It's not a bad place to meet. I don't expect any of the bad guys to attack me in a church."

"Are you afraid?" he asked.

Not something she wanted to admit. Alyssa opened her eyes and focused on him. "Did you go to church when you were growing up?"

"My family is Catholic. Nana Lucille took me to St. Louis Cathedral."

An incredible building with triple steeples, sky-high vaulted ceilings, ornate carvings and statuary, St. Louis was a symbol of culture in Louisiana, one of the oldest cathedrals in the country. She was reminded that, unlike her, he came from a traditional family with deep roots. Maybe he'd grown up in a mansion with pillars that looked like Tara. "Do you still have family in town?"

"Not anymore."

She sensed there might be an interesting story about the Fournier clan, but she didn't want to hear too much about Rafe or get too close. He had charm, an enticing grin and silver-gray eyes that sparkled and flashed. But she didn't dare trust him. Not until she understood what he was really after. Not until he shared the identity of his mysterious client.

Headed toward the Ninth Ward, he drove on

mostly deserted streets toward the bridge across the Mississippi and the canal. "I want to hear more about you, *cher*. You never finished your story about why you're in WitSec."

She'd been hoping to avoid reliving the actual murder. She could have gone on and on about Mr. Horowitz and how much she'd liked working for him. "Where did I stop talking?"

"You had explained your job."

"Right," she said. "By the time I graduated from high school, I decided that I wanted to be an accountant, a CPA, which meant I needed to get a degree. Mr. Horowitz agreed to pay for my college if I promised to continue working for him for four more years after college."

"A fair offer."

She agreed. "He's a really good person. I guess, maybe, I suspected that he was a fence. But is that so terrible? It's not that different from an auction?"

"But it is," he said. "A fence usually handles stolen goods."

"Don't patronize me." An irritated sigh puffed through her lips. "What I'm trying to say is that a lot of the jewelry that gets sold in a nasty divorce might as well be stolen. The same goes for expensive works of art used to pay gambling debts."

"Possession is assigned by law."

And she believed in the law. "You're right, but I hate to think of Mr. Horowitz doing anything illegal. It made me furious when the FBI agents questioned me and kept insisting that he committed fraud and laundered money. According to them, the fact that he'd disappeared after the murders was proof that he'd ripped off his clients."

"Did they have other evidence?" Rafe asked.

"Nothing but vague accusations." She hated their lies and how those suggestions implicated her. "Mr. Horowitz was kind and generous. I saw him give two thousand dollars to a widow who had to pawn her husband's Purple Heart. Later in the day, he arranged for the medal to be returned to her."

"It's possible to be a decent human being and a criminal at the same time."

"Is it?"

"I should know," he said. "My ancestors were pirates."

"Those guys in the FBI are so damned self-righteous. Again and again, they asked if I might have made an accounting mistake. Of course I might have. It's called human error. I didn't always balance to the penny. But they were talking about a ridiculous sum—seven million, six hundred thousand dollars."

He stomped the brake, whipped to the side

of the road, tore off his Ray-Bans and glared at her. "Repeat."

She did so and added, "I never should have told you."

"Au contraire." His unshaven jaw clenched. "That money is a powerful motive. It gives over seven and a half million reasons why those guys are after you and why they need to take you alive. They think you know where the money is."

"They're wrong."

"They might also be after your boss. Do you know where to find him?"

She lifted her chin to confront him. "Even if I did, I'd never tell."

He rattled off a long string of French phrases, some of which she recognized as curse words. Then he put the SUV in gear and merged into traffic. "Do you remember the names of any of the agents who questioned you about the money?"

"There were a bunch of them in Chicago and in court. Be more specific."

"What about the locals?" he asked. "Have you spoken to Agent Darren Jessop?"

"Tall and muscle-bound, blond hair and baby blue eyes," she said with a nod. "I remember him. The guy looks like he works out three times a day. Do you think he's after me? Working with Woodbridge?"

Instead of answering, Rafe stared straight ahead through the windshield as he drove onto the bridge. "Finish your story. I might as well know it all."

The dark waters of the river stretched as far as she could see on either side. So many secrets roiled beneath the surface. She'd confided in Rafe. *A mistake?* It felt like he knew more than she did and therefore had an advantage. They needed to be on equal footing. "I told you about the money. Now it's your turn. Why are you interested in Darren Jessop?"

"He knows my client, the man who hired me to protect you." He looked toward her. "I had hoped to talk with Jessop today."

"In person?"

"Or on the phone." His shrug had a touch of French nonchalance. "Back to your story. You claim that your job was not dangerous. And yet, you witnessed a shooting."

"Not in the pawnshop. My upstairs office was totally protected and private. I didn't deal with the people who came to pawn their treasures, and I didn't mess around with the merchandise. Other people did the stocking and made sure everything went where it was supposed to go."

"What was the regular procedure?"

"Lots of stuff was kept at the store, especially if Mr. Horowitz thought the person who pawned it was coming back. There was a huge walk-in safe downstairs, but much of the valuable stuff was stored at a separate location, a warehouse in Bedford Park."

In her mind's eye, Alyssa saw the neighborhood, which wasn't gritty but wasn't gentrified like the Fulton River Warehouse District. The warehouse used by the pawnshop was a square two-story redbrick building with a two-bay loading dock. Unremarkable on the outside, but the inside had been broken down into smaller containers with clean, white walls. These enclosed spaces were humidity and temperature controlled to maintain the artworks in peak condition and to keep the wood on antique furniture from warping. Walking among these containers had reminded her of a labyrinth.

Memory crept over her, and she shuddered. The air-conditioning in the SUV felt icy cold. She didn't want to talk about this. They exited the bridge, and Rafe drove east.

"Are we almost there?" she asked.

"We have enough time for you to finish your story," he said. "Tell me what happened at the warehouse."

"I hardly ever went there. In the five years I worked for Mr. Horowitz, I'd gone to the warehouse only ten or fifteen times by myself. On that day, I was checking balances in the ledgers against inventory sheets for an audit, and I discovered a discrepancy."

"How large was this discrepancy?"

"At the time, I thought it was huge, close to twenty thousand dollars, and I figured it had to be a mistake—*my* mistake. I was juggling a heavy schedule in college while working full-time, and I was exhausted. I didn't want to think I'd written the numbers wrong, and I hoped this was a simple matter of merchandise being misplaced in the warehouse. Mr. Horowitz was out of town, and I figured I could clean up the error before he came back."

As the memory became clear, she went silent. If she'd stayed in her office behind her desk, none of this would have happened. But she'd been full of herself, thought she could fix the problem with a wave of her hand. *Wrong, wrong, wrong.*

"Tell me about the discrepancy," he said.

"When I got to the warehouse, I should have known right away that something wasn't right. Frankie Leone, the warehouse supervisor, wasn't behind his desk. At the time, I was glad to slip inside unnoticed."

"Did you say Leone—Frankie Leone?"

She nodded. "Do you know him?"

"Continue with your story," he said. "You were glad to be unnoticed because you hoped to correct the discrepancy without anyone finding out."

She wished he'd stop saying *discrepancy.* It was her choice of word, and she hated herself for trying to be aloof, trying to turn her twenty-thousand-dollar mistake into something less stupid. "I botched things up, okay? If I hadn't gone to the warehouse, Ray McGill and his brother would have cleaned up the body and gotten away with murder. But I was there. I was a witness."

"Not your fault, *cher.*"

"Then why do I feel guilty down to my bones?"

"This was a large warehouse, yes? What kind of outsize items were stored there?"

"Construction equipment, motorcycles and vintage cars," she said. "Once I saw a speedboat."

"Do you know Diamond Jim Davidoff?"

"Everybody knows Diamond Jim. I bought a used Honda from him."

"And so? You are personally acquainted?"

She shook her head. "He's much too important to work on the lot, but I shook his hand at a fund-raising event. When I called his office about buying a car, he passed the word to the car salesman that I was a special customer."

"Continue your story, *s'il vous plaît*."

"I wandered through the containers until I found the wall safe where furs, designer gowns and jewelry were stored along with small antiques like clocks and lamps. I used the combination, opened the door and went inside the ventilated, temperature-controlled safe. That's when I heard gunshots."

And her heart had stopped. She hadn't wanted to believe that the popping noise was gunfire and went to the door of the safe to look out. "A man staggered toward me. His sweatshirt was covered with blood. When he got closer, I recognized him as Frankie Leone. Before he collapsed in my arms, I saw Ray McGill shoot him one more time. I grabbed Frankie and shut the door to the safe. It automatically locked."

"And you were trapped inside with Frankie Leone, a man who was dying."

She appreciated the way he mentioned the name of the dying man. The FBI agents and the marshals had always referred to him as the "victim." Not acknowledging his given identity seemed to diminish his passing. "There was so much blood. I could tell that he was in pain. His eyes squeezed shut. He passed out."

Every time she spoke of those helpless, painful, terrible moments, Alyssa felt one step closer to death. She'd called 911 on her cell phone and managed to get a tenuous connection before the phone went dead. Desperately, she'd needed to believe that help was on the way, but she didn't know for sure. Frankie Leone lay unconscious in her arms. How to save him? She tried to remember first aid. Was she supposed to wake him? Or put pressure on the wound? She didn't know CPR but had seen it done.

When she pushed up his sweatshirt, any thought of pushing on his chest was erased. Blood oozed from his wounds. He'd been shot several times. From outside the safe, she heard more gunshots, which had to be McGill and his pals trying to break inside. She wrapped Frankie in a full-length mink coat to make him comfortable.

"He never opened his eyes," she said. "His breathing stilled, and then it stopped. The police took over an hour to arrest McGill and get the safe opened. By then, Frankie had started to turn cold."

She'd held him tightly. Though Frankie was beyond help, she'd wanted to protect him. This might be the hundredth time she'd told this story, but it never got easier.

To her surprise, Rafe reached across the console, placed his hand on her forearm and gave a gentle squeeze. He didn't say anything, but the physical contact soothed her. The warmth of his hand melted the chill that had enveloped her body.

When she looked up at him, she could tell that he had experienced a similar trauma. They didn't need words to communicate. Coming close to violent death had changed her forever, and she was certain that he felt the same way. If she hadn't been strapped in by her seat belt, she would have climbed across the console and wrapped her arms around him, pressing herself against him so she could absorb his heat and his strength.

He pulled over to a curb and parked.

"Are we at the church?" she asked.

He nodded.

She'd been so distracted by the telling of her story that she hadn't noticed their surroundings. The Ninth Ward had been devastated by Katrina when the levees broke, and parts of the area still looked like a war zone. Other streets—like this one—had been rebuilt and replanted. The road itself was in need of repair, but the homes on either side were tidy frame houses, some painted with bright colors. She noticed a one-story house with purple and yellow stripes. The church took up several lots on the corner and had a parking lot, which Rafe had chosen to ignore.

The rebuilt church had a simple design with

a white steeple. Along both sides were tall, narrow windows with gray hurricane shutters. Behind the main building, she saw a patio with a barbecue and a garden. A long, low one-story structure, probably a recreation hall, stood on the other side of the patio. The church entrance was up two wide stairs and had an arched double door made of heart pine. Two women stood outside talking. One was black, the other white, and both wore sundresses.

Alyssa pulled herself together. "I'm ready."

"If we encounter danger," he said, "we leave. *Immédiatement.* Do you understand?"

"I get it. The bad guys might recognize me. I know my disguise is distracting, but I'm not invisible."

He came around to the passenger side and opened the car door for her like a gentleman. She was equally ladylike in her Baby Doll pink with the rhinestone sunglasses. She took his arm as they strolled up the sidewalk. The clean concrete looked like it had been recently poured.

Though the Peace and Hope Church seemed to live up to the nonthreatening name, a shiver of fear twitched across her shoulder blades. "We could be walking into a trap."

He didn't deny her statement as they strolled toward the church doors, one of which was opened. From inside, they heard clapping and singing as "If I Can Dream" came to an end. With a polite nod to the ladies at the door who handed out programs, Rafe escorted her inside. They stood at the rear and watched as the congregation got comfortable in the pews.

In the raised sanctuary at the front, the pastor—a handsome, barrel-chested man in a double-breasted burgundy suit—strutted back and forth behind the railing. His energy couldn't be confined to the pulpit; this man had to move. His speaking cadence was rhythmic, almost musical, and he reminded her of speakers who had come to her family's church in Savannah.

The design of the sanctuary was simple with little more than a cross, a pulpit and benches for the choir. But the decorations were plentiful, including tall bouquets of dahlias and mums and fragrant roses. The floral scent mingled with the waxy smell from yellow, green and orange candles of every shape and size. Hanging from the overhead beams, embroidered banners displayed messages of love and friendship. The pastor wrapped up his message, and the choir, dressed in burnt-orange robes, rose to their feet.

Peace and Hope was actually very similar to her childhood church, with a diverse congregation and plain decorations instead of statuary. Still, Alyssa was surprised when the pastor spoke of her church and introduced the visiting soloist as a member from that congregation. Her name was unfamiliar.

The organ player hit the opening chords, and a woman stepped away from the others in the choir. She stood tall, her hands clasped at her breast. Her curly silver hair was tucked into a bun on the top of her head.

Frozen in place, Alyssa stared. This woman could have been her mom. She had the same high forehead, the same wide-set eyes. When she sang, her soprano resonated with the same compelling vibrato as Alyssa's mom, Claudia. That voice filled the sanctuary and the nave and flowed out the door all the way to the street. "Amazing Grace" would live forever in Alyssa's fondest memories. She closed her eyes and imagined that her mom was still living, thriving and having a chance at happiness. But that was a lie. Mom was dead. Alyssa had seen her in the coffin, had wept at her grave.

The silver-haired woman currently raising her voice in song was, most likely, the anonymous caller who had summoned them to the church. But that wasn't all. This woman was presumed dead ten years ago, though her body was never found. For better or worse, this beloved and infuriating woman was Alyssa's aunt Charlotte.

Chapter Nine

The shock of seeing her aunt crashed into Alyssa with a paralyzing force that rattled her bones and twisted her muscles in knots. *This can't be! Aunt Charlotte is dead!* She was so tense that when Rafe touched her shoulder, Alyssa bolted away from him like a scared rabbit, darted across the back of the church and cowered in the corner. Her heart beat louder than the sonorous voice of the pastor as he directed his congregation to the next hymn.

Rafe eased up beside her and whispered, "Should we go?"

"Not until I talk to her." Somehow, she had to figure out what had happened ten years ago. And why, oh why, had Charlotte returned now? *I don't understand.* Alyssa wasn't rational, couldn't think.

"Who is she?"

She was surprised that he didn't know. "My aunt Charlotte."

"The one who is dead?"

She nodded. When Charlotte died...or disappeared... Mom had been devastated. Alyssa had been unable to assuage the grief they both felt. Even now, ten years later, she experienced the loss. A sob crawled up her throat, but now was not the time for an outburst. She pressed a hand over her mouth to stifle her sorrow.

Rafe took her other hand. "Come with me."

Her initial horror was beginning to ebb, leaving her numb. "I'm scared."

"You were right, *cher*, when you said we need to talk to her. Why is she here? What does she want?" He squeezed her hand and gave a tug. "It must be important. Why else would she return from the dead?"

Being with Rafe boosted her courage. With him at her side, she could move forward. She had to know why Charlotte was here and what kind of game she was playing.

The Hope and Peace congregation—filled with the spirit—sang "Wade in the Water" with gusto and hand clapping, barely noticing as Rafe guided her down the aisle under the windows. In spite of the emotional chaos that raged within her, she found herself humming along with the old-time spiritual, a familiar touchstone. When she was a kid, she'd stood in the front pew and belted out hymns in her imperfect alto while her mom and her aunt stood on either side of her and sang like angels.

When they approached the altar rail, Charlotte gestured to them and moved toward an exit at the back of the sanctuary. Rafe led Alyssa past the choir into a hallway. A door at the end stood open.

Before entering the room, he scanned the hallway. His jacket was pulled back, revealing his weapon, and she remembered that he was a bodyguard. They needed to be vigilant. The innocent-looking congregation might be harboring a snake—three snakes, to be more precise, Woodbridge and his two companions. Was Charlotte working with them? Would she hesitate for one minute before throwing her niece under the bus?

On one level, Alyssa was happy that her aunt was alive and well. No longer alone in the world, she had family again. But she was also furious. Charlotte had chosen to leave. Faking her death was bad enough, but she'd made it a hundred times worse by choosing to stay away from them. When her mom died, Alyssa could have used the loving support of her aunt, but Charlotte couldn't be bothered to come home.

Alyssa stalked toward the open door. "Let's get this over with."

"I'll go first," Rafe said as he drew his weapon.

She followed him into a plain, windowless room that seemed to be used for storage and changing clothes. Tidy but musty, there were cardboard boxes on the floor. Shelves and cabinets lined the walls. Choir robes in burnt orange, burgundy and green hung from metal racks.

Standing with her back to a full-length mirror, Charlotte waited for them. Over six feet tall in her high heels, she was long limbed and chic in a sleeveless black dress with a heavy gold necklace. Her generous mouth stretched in a grin, and she held her arms wide. "Come to me, my sweet niece."

Alyssa caught her breath. "No."

"Why not?"

"I can't forgive and forget. Not without an explanation." She was hurt and angry. Surely, that was understandable. There had been many gallons of water under this bridge. "The last time I saw you, I was sixteen. And you were a brunette."

The platinum and silver bun on top of Charlotte's head was coming undone. Wispy curls tumbled artlessly and encircled her face. She pointed a long, bony finger at Alyssa's blond wig. "At least I'm not trying to be a princess."

"Neither am I." Princess was a game they'd played when she was a little girl. Aunt Charlotte was the best when it came to imagination and dress-up. Real life wasn't her thing.

"Remember?" Her voice held a teasing note. "We had to slay the dragon."

"I'm not dressed up like this for fun and games. This wig is a disguise I'm wearing because somebody is trying to abduct me." Resentment bubbled up inside her. "I suppose you know all about that."

"Why would I?"

"You called and invited me to the *Día de los Muertos* parade. Am I right? Was that you?"

"So what if it was?"

"At the parade, you signaled me and I got attacked. Coincidence?" Alyssa didn't dare take off her sunglasses; she didn't want her tears to show. "Who are you working for, Charlotte? I hope they're paying you enough to make it worthwhile. What's the going rate for betraying your family?"

"I'm disappointed in you, Lara."

"I don't use that name anymore."

"After what you've been through with WitSec, I thought you'd understand the terrible problems that have plagued my life. For ten years, I've been in hiding—a woman without a home. Not that it's been all bad. I have enough cash and assets to get by, and my singing career is doing fairly well."

"You sing in public," Rafe said. "That doesn't seem like hiding."

"You're not a pro, so I wouldn't expect you to understand. In every big city, there are dozens of dreadfully anonymous piano bars. When I hook up with a band, I can sing at weddings and parties. If I didn't have to keep such a low profile, I could be a star."

Alyssa gave a snort. "Yeah, sure, just like I could be a princess."

"Don't sass me. I did what was necessary to survive. Sometimes, it's best to run away and live to fight another day."

"Where did you learn that? From a fortune cookie?"

Rafe inserted himself between them, spreading his natural charm like a healing balm on this most horrendous of family reunions. He introduced himself to her aunt and said, "I know your first name is Charlotte. What's your last name?"

"Take your pick," she said with a toss of her head. "Do you want my maiden name or my surname from one of my three marriages? Or maybe I should give you one of my aliases."

"I get it," he said. "Your life is complicated, and you have much to discuss with your niece, but now is not the time for a chat. The church might not be safe for her."

Her green eyes narrowed. "I'd never do anything that would put Alyssa in danger."

"Why are you here?" he asked.

"In the Ninth Ward at this church? I knew the pastor and contacted him when I got into town. He invited me to do a solo. I'm not getting paid, but I never turn down a gig."

"I meant," Rafe said, "why are you in New Orleans?"

"To contact Lara or Alyssa or whatever she's calling herself. I had hoped we'd meet at the parade." Her head swiveled toward Alyssa. "We missed connections."

Or maybe Charlotte's call was an excuse to draw her into danger. "Your phone call came from Anonymous. Why didn't you identify yourself?"

Charlotte rolled her eyes like a disgruntled teenager. "I figured it was better to meet for the first time in person. If I announced myself on the phone, it would have been a shock."

"Did you think it would be better to pop up like a returned-from-the-dead, zombie jack-in-the-box?"

"Sarcasm is such an unattractive quality."

"So is stupidity." Alyssa didn't want to be mean but couldn't help herself. "What did you think would happen when I saw you on the street?"

"A warm hug? A kiss on both cheeks?"

"I thought you were Mom's ghost. You scared me out of my skin." Alyssa shook her head. "Enough of these guessing games, just tell me the truth. Are you working with Woodbridge?"

"Who's that?" Her eyes widened in what might have been an innocent expression, if this woman had been capable of truth or sincerity. "I've never heard that name."

"Who wanted you to come to New Orleans and find me?"

"I can't tell you."

Alyssa turned on her heel and took two long strides toward the door. She felt her aunt's gaze boring a hole in her spine, but she didn't look back. "I admire your ability to survive, Charlotte. And when it comes to singing, you're incredible. But there's more to life than talent and money. You hurt me, and you hurt Mom."

"What about me? My pain? It wasn't easy to walk away. Yes, I lied, but I've paid the price. My life has been a living hell."

Alyssa paused with her hand on the doorknob. "Why did you do it?"

"If I had stayed in Chicago, they would have killed me and probably would have come after you and Claudia. It was my fault. I doublecrossed Frankie Leone."

Alyssa whirled to face her. Frankie Leone

was the man who had died in her arms. She glanced at Rafe and saw a similar recognition on his face. Alyssa cleared her throat. "Keep talking."

"I was dating Frankie. I think he was involved with the McGill crime family, the same guys who are after you. In his apartment, I found a stash of money and merchandise that he was holding for them, and I gambled it away. Frankie tried to protect me, but I had to disappear—just like you had to change your identity in witness protection."

Alyssa asked, "How did you manage to escape?"

"I had a few powerful friends." She twined her hands at her breast—a dramatic gesture. "They helped me fake my death in that fire. One of them arranged transportation and set up an account to pay my living expenses."

Now we're getting somewhere! Alyssa demanded, "Who was this friend?"

"He made me promise never to tell anyone, especially not you."

Alyssa couldn't think of a single reason why her aunt's secret benefactor would single her out. Until the moment when she accidentally stumbled over a murder, she'd been a quiet accountant who juggled numbers and kept to herself.

"Your benefactor," Rafe said, "did he send

you on this trip to New Orleans to find your niece?"

"Yes."

"What does he want from her?"

"Information." Charlotte exhaled a dramatic sigh. "A large sum of money has gone missing, and he thinks Alyssa might know something about it. Listen, I'm one hundred percent sure that he means no harm. He's basically a good, decent person."

As if Charlotte was a good judge of character? Alyssa wasn't buying this story. If this decent person had nothing to hide, why didn't he just call her? Why set up this elaborate ruse? "You can tell your so-called friend that I don't know anything about the seven million, six hundred thousand dollars, which is exactly what I told the FBI and WitSec."

"Can I see you again?"

"There was a time when I would have done anything to be with you again." Alyssa steeled herself inside. "But I don't need you anymore. I'm totally independent. I've learned how to take care of myself."

"I used to think the same thing. And I used to be just as proud as you are. That was before I spent ten years moving from place to place, always looking over my shoulder. I couldn't put down roots or make friends. There were times when I would have traded all my talent and my money to be normal—just a normal woman who could fall in love. When you're on the run, you can't trust anyone. Without trust, you can't build a relationship." She glanced back and forth between them. "I envy you, sweetheart. I could never have what you and Rafe have."

"What? Me and Rafe? We're not a couple."

A knowing smile curled Charlotte's lips. "I see the way he looks at you. And I caught you looking back."

Before Alyssa could voice another objection, Rafe stepped into the conversation. "I have two questions, Charlotte. First, do you know Diamond Jim Davidoff?"

"Sure, everybody does."

"Was he one of your special friends?"

"The last I heard, Diamond Jim was too busy running his auto scams to mess around with anything else."

"Second question," Rafe said. "Is Darren Jessop one of your associates?"

"Special Agent Jessop? As a matter of fact, he's a pal. When I first got to New Orleans, he set me up with a place to stay."

"Does he know you're here at this church?"

"I'm not sure."

"I'll take that as a yes," Rafe said. "Therefore, we must say adieu."

Alyssa allowed herself to be propelled from the room without saying a proper goodbye to her aunt. Charlotte was mistaken in thinking that she and Rafe had a relationship. He was her bodyguard, nothing more. Why would she even consider her aunt's opinion? The woman's life was one terrible decision after another, and she was wrong about almost everything. Alyssa couldn't pinpoint the lies in Charlotte's story, but she was certain that her aunt hadn't told the whole truth.

Rafe hustled her out a rear door that opened onto the garden between the church and the recreation hall. Members of the flock were drinking coffee and nibbling on homemade muffins and cookies. It was a charming, normal scene on a pleasant Sunday morning that contrasted the wild, jagged emotions tearing through her. She and Rafe moved away from the crowd, nearly running.

In seconds, they were in his SUV. As he pulled away from the curb, she pressed her back into her seat and inhaled a deep breath, struggling to release her tension. "Is somebody after us?"

"It's possible, *cher.*"

"As soon as Charlotte mentioned Agent Jessop, you dashed out the door. Do you think he's here?"

"I do," he said. "Jessop has been in touch with Charlotte since she came to the city, and he's FBI. That means he has her under surveillance and is tracking her movements."

She realized that he was speaking from personal experience. "Is that what you would have done when you were a fed?"

"It's standard procedure."

"Similar to the way you followed me." For more than two weeks, he'd been on her tail, and she hadn't noticed him lurking in the shadows. Rafe was clever and skilled. There was no way she should trust this pirate. And yet… "Jessop is a federal agent, right?"

"Correct."

"Why do you think he's dangerous?"

"I don't know, but it could be for the same reason that Marshal Woodbridge dressed like a skeleton and tried to kidnap you."

"The money?"

"Possibly."

When it came to keeping her in the dark, he was as bad as her aunt Charlotte. They played their games and left her feeling like an idiot. She ripped off her sunglasses, took a tissue from her purse and confronted her image in the visor mirror. Her leaky tears had destroyed her eyeliner and mascara. "I should have figured out what was going on with Charlotte. But how could

I? She was supposed to be dead. How could I guess that my aunt was on the run? What kind of crazy lady fakes her death and disappears?"

He guided the SUV to a stop at a red light and turned toward her. "She's not altogether different from you. Your plan is to run—to disappear by using aliases and disguises."

His comparison was accurate. Like Charlotte, she planned to leave New Orleans and move to a different location where she'd take on a new identity. She'd start over and find a way to survive, trusting no one, taking care of herself. For years, her identity had been based on those principles of self-sufficiency, but her plan had never felt so lonely.

Aunt Charlotte was a cautionary tale, and Alyssa didn't want to dive down the same rabbit hole.

Chapter Ten

Without a clear destination in mind, Rafe drove in a northeastern direction while he observed the traffic in his rearview mirror, making sure they'd escaped the church without picking up a tail. The similarities between Alyssa and her aunt had not been wasted on him. Though he suspected that Charlotte had always been a borderline criminal and Alyssa seemed to have a clear grasp of right and wrong, they were both stubborn, fiercely independent and determined to take care of themselves.

His thinking was colored by how much he'd come to like Alyssa after observing her for sixteen days. More than her green-eyed beauty, he appreciated her spirit and her intelligence. She could think fast, which was sometimes a blessing and sometimes a curse. Her impulse to chase after the skeletons had almost led to her capture.

Likewise, her independence held an element

of danger. She trusted no one. He hated to think of the deep disappointments she must have experienced to build such a solid fortress around her heart. From the early abandonment by her father to the current debacle with Aunt Charlotte, Alyssa had been duped and discarded. No one stood beside her. Even her mom was gone. And Max Horowitz, her kindly boss who helped her through college, had disappeared.

Rafe couldn't expect her to trust him, but he had to keep her safe. Not only was that the job he'd been hired to do, but he cared for her. The real question was: Should he hand her over to the FBI? Law enforcement could protect her better than he could...if they hadn't been corrupted like Woodbridge.

After driving a few more aimless miles, he was certain that they were being followed. And he had a pretty good idea who was driving the bronze sedan with the tinted windows. Rafe cranked the steering wheel and made an unexpected left turn. The sedan dodged through traffic to follow.

Alyssa yelped from the passenger seat. "What are you doing?"

"Shaking a tail."

Any attempt to outsmart Jessop with defensive-driving techniques seemed futile. They had both been given the same training at the FBI.

Each could anticipate the other's moves. The best way to escape was luck, the whims of traffic and skills Rafe had picked up when he was undercover as a race car driver.

"Is it Jessop?" Alyssa guessed.

"Probably."

"But that isn't a bad thing. Over breakfast, you mentioned setting up a meeting with him to get more information. What changed your mind?"

"It's hard to say."

During the few months Rafe had been part of the New Orleans office of the FBI, he was mostly undercover and out of contact with the other agents. He didn't know Jessop well, but he didn't want to poison Alyssa's mind against him in case it was necessary to transfer her into FBI custody.

She twisted her shoulders, craned her neck and peered through the rear window of the SUV. "Is he still following us?"

"I don't see him," Rafe said, "but he could be behind that truck."

"You asked both me and Charlotte about Jessop and about Diamond Jim Davidoff. There's a connection between them, right?"

She was too intelligent to believe an ill-formed lie. "Yes."

"I'm guessing that Jessop—an FBI agent who

knows you—was the person who referred Diamond Jim to you. That means that Mr. Davidoff is your client."

"Now that you've solved that mystery, I have another—"

"It's not solved," she said. "Not until I know why Davidoff hired you to be my bodyguard. His interest is probably motivated by the seven million, six hundred thousand dollars, but that doesn't explain why he wanted the decor to look like my bedroom."

"A talk for later." He set the conversation aside, hoping to distract her. "We have a different issue. Jessop is back."

"Which car?"

"The bronze Lexus."

"How can you tell? I can't identify the driver through the tinted window."

"An assumption," he said. "I remember the car from when we worked together, and I can't think of anyone else who could have followed us from the church."

With a sigh, she said, "There are just so damn many bad guys."

"As long as you trust me, we'll be okay."

He expected her response to be the oft-repeated statement of being able to take care of herself, and so he was surprised when she reached across the console and touched his arm. "Trust is important."

"It is, *cher.*"

"That stuff Charlotte said about you and me wasn't true, was it?" Her fingers lightly squeezed his forearm. "I'm not interested in a relationship. Are you?"

"I'm French," he reminded her. "I'm always interested."

"Okay." She withdrew her hand. "How do you plan to meet with Jessop? If you pull over and let him catch up with us, he's going to grab me and sweep me into custody."

"You're right." And there was no one else in the local office that he implicitly trusted. Much of his undercover career had been in Florida until a long-term investigation into a smuggling ring had blown up in his face. That was one of the reasons he'd decided to quit the FBI.

"I don't want to go back to the house and hide. What if Jessop tracks us there?"

Again, he agreed with her reading of the situation. He couldn't leave her alone and unguarded at the house. But he couldn't allow her to meet Jessop in person. "I know a place where you can be part of the conversation but protected at the same time."

"And where is this magical place?"

"St. Louis Cemetery Number Three on Esplanade."

Over the years, Rafe had used the aboveground cemetery as a rendezvous for informants, suspects and—once or twice—girlfriends. His family had a mausoleum, and he knew his way around the place. As a kid he'd played hide-and-seek among the tombs during the interment of an aged uncle or a reckless cousin.

"Let me get this straight." Alyssa cast a skeptical gaze in his direction. "You think a graveyard is a safe meeting place?"

A simple "trust me" wasn't going to ease her mind. "Allow me to explain with a short history of St. Louis Cemetery and my family."

"By all means."

"Cemetery Number Three opened in 1854, and the Fournier mausoleum was built two years later. My pirate ancestor, Jean-Pierre, had passed away in 1812, leaving his family with treasure but not respectability. His wife argued with the priests about burial for her husband in the existing cemeteries and decided on a more humble resting place. By the time Cemetery Number Three was laid out, the Fournier family was solidly established in New Orleans society, and one of my aunts wanted a big, showy, ornate monument."

"Your roots go deep," she said.

"*Oui.* There are so few of us left."

"I still don't know why you want to meet with Jessop in the cemetery."

"Every soul in New Orleans knows where the cemetery is located, and the Fournier mausoleum stands out. The walls are sun-bleached marble. Above the entrance is a peaked arch with a frieze of a sailing ship flying the Jolly Roger. Posed on top is a statue of a winged angel with a sword."

"Got it," she said. "It's easy to find."

"At the cemetery, I have an edge—an all-access parking sticker that allows me to drive onto the grounds. Also, most important, I have a key to the Fournier monument."

"Why's the key a big deal?"

"While I talk with Jessop, you will be safely locked inside the mausoleum."

"With dead people?" Her voice elevated several octaves. "Oh, I don't think so. Not that I believe in ghosts or zombies."

"At present there is no coffin in the tomb."

"If there's no coffin, who's buried there?"

Not wanting to give her another reason to be nervous, he decided not to go into details about the process of interment—waiting for the corpse to decompose, removing the coffin and returning the bones to the mausoleum. The remains of at least thirty-two people were housed in his family's mausoleum. "No need to be afraid, *cher*. The Fournier dead are very well behaved."

"Look at my face, Rafe. I'm not laughing."

She folded her arms across her middle and sank down in the passenger seat. With her long blond wig and pink dress, she looked like an angry sunbeam. He hadn't expected Alyssa—a down-to-earth accountant who planned for everything—to be superstitious. But he trusted her ability to cope. Meeting Jessop at the Fournier tomb was a good solution.

Without further discussion, he used his hands-free phone to connect with the number he had for Jessop. Rafe wanted to keep this conversation and the subsequent meeting short and simple. His plan was to use Jessop to find out who was after Alyssa and what they wanted from her.

As soon as Jessop answered, Rafe said, "Stop tailing me."

"Why would I be interested in following you?"

"In your bronze Lexus," he said. "In three blocks, I intend to merge onto the bridge. If you follow, we won't meet. If you do as I say, I'll arrange to sit down for a brief parley."

"Who's the girl, Rafe? Who's the blonde that followed you out of the church? I know Alyssa is a brunette, but she could have been wearing a wig."

"Don't follow."

As Rafe disconnected the call, she pulled the blond curls off her head and combed through her sienna-brown hair with her fingers. "So much for my Baby Doll disguise."

"It served the purpose," he said as he drove onto the bridge. "Look through the back window. Can you see the Lexus?"

When she unfastened her seat belt and leaned over to look through the seats, her arm brushed his shoulder, and he felt an electric surge. Her crazy aunt had been strangely accurate when she predicted a relationship—not that he was looking for anything long term, but he wanted to go deep and know her in a meaningful way.

"I don't see Jessop," she said.

"If we're lucky, he's already stopped following us."

Rafe checked his rearview mirror, making sure they weren't being followed. On the other side of the bridge, he parked the SUV on a side street and called Jessop again. The FBI special agent answered quickly and started talking right away, issuing demands and threats. His technique failed to impress Rafe. They'd gone through the same interrogation training.

He cut through Jessop's chatter with a terse instruction. "Meet me at the Fournier mausoleum in St. Louis Cemetery Number Three at noon."

"That doesn't give me enough time."

"This is your only chance, *mon ami*."

Rafe ended the call and turned to Alyssa. "You were smart to bring your backpack."

"I like to be well prepared and organized. It's what I do." She cracked open the passenger door. "I bet you want me to climb into the back and change out of this glaring outfit into something more subtle."

"S'il vous plaît."

As soon as she got into the back of the SUV, he redirected his route toward Esplanade Avenue. Situated between Lake Pontchartrain and St. John's Bayou, Cemetery Number Three had been badly flooded during Hurricane Katrina, leading to horror stories—mostly untrue—about floating coffins and decomposing corpses. These were not tales he'd pass along to Alyssa.

Glancing into the rearview mirror, he had a partial view of her shoulder and her lacy white bra before she slipped into a blue T-shirt and a denim jacket. Last night when he rescued her from the skeletons and had to remove her clothing, he'd seen more of her body. But she'd been unconscious. This glimpse was more exciting. Even the khaki shorts seemed sexy.

He tore his gaze away from the mirror and concentrated on what needed to come next. He had promised Davidoff that he would send a photo of Alyssa by noon today in order to prove that she was alive and well and not captured by Woodbridge or anyone else.

Davidoff remained a puzzle. His concern for Alyssa, the fact that he'd hired Rafe to protect her and his insistence on making her comfortable with a bedroom decorated like her own seemed like the actions of someone who cared about her—the father who had stepped out of her life but continued to love her? Charlotte probably could have explained Davidoff's interest in her niece, but she chose to keep her secrets.

"I'm ready." Alyssa poked her head between the front seats. "It took a million wet wipes to get the goopy makeup off my face, but I'm clean."

"I like your face without makeup."

She patted his cheek. "And I like your scruffy look. Are we almost there?"

"In a minute."

"Should I duck down and hide?"

"Couldn't hurt."

He'd taken the quickest route and doubted that Jessop could have arrived before him, but there was always the possibility that the FBI agent was working with someone else. Keeping Alyssa hidden from the feds, her crazy aunt and Davidoff was vital. If no one knew where she was, they couldn't hurt her.

Chapter Eleven

Crouched down in the back seat of the SUV, Alyssa tried to regain the emotional balance and determination she'd lost when she came face-to-face with her aunt…her dead aunt. *Impossible! Everything has turned upside down.* Her plan to leave town and start over seemed less positive and more futile. The example of Charlotte's wasted life reminded her that escape was impossible. The bad stuff would catch up, no matter where she ran.

What was her alternative? She couldn't stay here and wait for Woodbridge or Jessop or anybody else to grab her. She needed another plan, and that meant gathering more information and hoping that something would make sense. The meeting with Agent Jessop seemed like a good starting place, but she wasn't real happy about the idea of hiding out in a tomb.

"We're here," Rafe said, "entering the City of the Dead."

"You don't have to sound so cheerful about it."

She raised her head just high enough to peek out the window as the SUV turned at the entrance to St. Louis Cemetery Number Three. Outside the curlicue wrought iron gate, piles of bouquets from last night's parade were stacked in remembrance. The flowers were already starting to rot, giving off a pungent odor that penetrated the car and overpowered the air-conditioning.

She pinched her nose. "Why are the flowers outside instead of on the graves?"

"The cemeteries used to stay open for All Souls' Day and Day of the Dead, but the celebrations got too wild and destructive, especially in Cemetery Number One, where the voodoo queen Marie Laveau is interred."

That site was supposed to have voodoo magic. "I heard that if you mark three X's on her tomb, she'll grant one wish."

"And so the desecration became standard practice. *C'est triste.* It's sad. I regret the lack of access for the general public, but I'm glad there will be no graffiti to scrub from the Fournier monument."

Alyssa crouched lower and pulled the backpack over her head and shoulders while the official at the gate checked Rafe's identification and waved him through. He drove slowly, dropping casual facts like someone who had given this tour many times before. "The layout in Number Three is more organized than in the other two, and the statuary and tombs are more elaborate. If you look on the left, you can see a nearly life-size bronze of Padre Pio, who was famous for his stigmata."

She peeked through the window as they drove on a narrow street—Rafe referred to it as an aisle—between rows of tombs that were roughly the size of camping trailers but made of marble and stone. "How many crypts are there?"

"Over ten thousand burial sites and more than three thousand wall vaults," he said, "plus a Greek Orthodox section and mausoleums housing nuns and priests who had no other place to be buried."

Flowers had been left outside the doors to many of the tombs, and the urns had been decorated with colorful displays of posies, feathers and beads. They drove past a woman and child who sat close together on a marble bench. Other people strolled along the aisle beside the grass border, not a crowd but a respectable number for a Sunday morning at the beginning of November. During her time in New Orleans, Alyssa had come to appreciate the city's acceptance of death as a celebration of the moment when a beloved person is freed from the bonds of earthly existence. Grief was inescapable, but Alyssa liked to imagine her mom at a wake filled with singing and dancing. Mom would have loved to have her coffin paraded in a jazz procession with trumpets, trombones and tambourines.

Carved stone tombs were much more interesting than being buried in the ground, but she still didn't want to be locked inside one. Peering through the car window, she nodded to a marble statue of a serene Virgin Mary with her hands outstretched and shot out a little prayer, asking for strength.

She cleared her throat. "How is Jessop going to find your family's tomb in the midst of all this?"

"As I mentioned before, it stands out." He parked the SUV. "Voilà!"

She sat up and stared. The Fournier tomb was, as promised, spectacular. Made of pale marble and rising several feet taller than either of its neighbors, the sepulchre had two slender columns flanking the double doors. The sword-wielding angel on top was ferocious with muscular arms and a mane of long, curly hair.

"That is some kind of tomb," she said as she emerged from the back seat.

"My great-great-great-great-aunt, who commissioned this monument, was red-hot furious when the priests excluded the descendants of the pirate Jean-Pierre Fournier from Cemetery Number One. She was determined to make a statement."

"She succeeded. Who's the angel on top?"

"Nana Lucille told me it's the archangel Rafael, my namesake. But I always thought it was Saint Peter. He had more to do with sailors."

She could easily imagine Rafe in the role of an avenging angel, diving into the fray with his flaming sword. If only she could trust him, life would be so much easier. But there had never been a time in her life when she had someone to lean on and be sure they'd support her. No doubt Rafe was as irresponsible as all the rest.

On the wall beside the door of the tomb, she noticed two vertical rows of engraved metal markers; there must have been more than thirty. Each marker had a name. "What do those names mean?"

"Those are the people buried in the tomb."

"Wait! You said nobody was in there." A flash of panic exploded inside her skull. "You promised there were no coffins."

"That's true."

"But all those people are buried in there."

"Try not to think about it, *cher*." He took her arm and moved her toward a poplar tree. "Stand here and act natural so I can take your picture for Davidoff."

"First, you need to explain." Her misgivings about entering the tomb had quadrupled. "After the coffins are removed, what happens to the corpses?"

"Nature takes its course," he said. "A body in a coffin sealed in a tomb and baking in the sun decomposes in a year or two. There's nothing left but the bones. In our family, we put the bones in a bag and return them to a marble ossuary at the back of the mausoleum."

Her throat closed, and she squeaked. "They're still in the tomb? Are we talking about the remains of thirty-something dead people?"

"You have nothing to fear, *cher.*" He gestured for her to stand by the tree. "Don't look in my direction."

"I don't want to be locked up with a bunch of ossuary bones."

"Let's get this photo."

Inhaling a deep breath, she tried to ground herself. "Why don't you want me to turn toward you for the picture?"

"Davidoff doesn't need to know that we're working together. I'll frame the photo so none of the tombs are visible and the location isn't obvious."

She placed her hand on a low-hanging tree branch and gazed into the distance—a pose that was typical of a senior photo in a high school album. Lifting a slight smile onto her lips, she tried to look like she wasn't with Rafe and wasn't in a graveyard. His mention of Davidoff was a distraction from the unreasonable terror of being locked up in the tomb. Diamond Jim gave her a very tangible reason to be scared. He was interested enough in her to hire a bodyguard, and he seemed to want her to feel comfortable in the copycat bedroom. *But why?*

Davidoff had to be after the money. Like everybody else, he probably believed that she had a clue. But she didn't. The fact that she didn't have the secret knowledge that would lead to the missing millions was a problem more terrifying than if she could hand over a map showing the location of the treasure. If she was caught by any of these other thugs, she had nothing to give them, nothing she could use to bargain her way to freedom.

"The picture is taken," he said. "Now, come with me. It's time to hide."

"There's only one reason I'm going along with this plan," she said as she walked toward him. "Jessop might have useful information, and I've got to figure out what's going on. I also have questions for you, starting with an explanation about Davidoff and the weirdly decorated room."

"But of course."

"I hope you're taking me seriously," she grumbled. "Promise you'll tell me."

"Shall I cross my heart? Pinkie swear?"

"Listen up, Mr. Pirate or Avenging Angel or whoever, if you want my trust, you're going to have to start telling me the truth."

"I could say the same to you."

Taken aback, she masked her reaction. Did he know her secret? No way—he couldn't possibly know. She hadn't told the FBI or the US marshals or anybody. As long as she was on this tightrope, balancing for dear life, she wouldn't give away her safety net. She watched Rafe bound up the two wide stairs to the door of the tomb. When he fitted the old-fashioned key into the lock, twisted and pushed the door open, she could have sworn that she heard an ominous creak.

"Is this really necessary?" she asked. "Why can't I hide in the back of the car?"

"Inside this marble monument, you'll be safe. Nobody can reach you."

She swallowed hard, trying not to think of every horror movie she'd ever seen about being buried alive. "How do I get out?"

"You'll have this." He held the antique key toward her, and she noticed the skull and cross-bones in the design at the top loop. "Not one of the originals, but it works just fine."

To illustrate, he leaned hard against the door on the left side. The carved wood appeared to be old and weathered enough to be part of the original 1856 construction. Sneaking around in this very old monument to the dead struck her as being somewhat irreverent.

Reaching into the pocket of his suit coat, Rafe lured her closer by holding up her cell phone. "You can have this back. I replaced some of the software and added encryption to make it impossible to trace your location. Don't turn it on unless you have to."

With a sense of satisfaction, she tucked the phone into the shoulder bag she'd brought from the car. Though she wasn't a person who spent every minute on social media, she'd felt naked without her phone. "Thank you."

He ushered her into the tomb and quickly lit three votive candles. The flickering light streaked against the roughened walls, where more than a century of dirt had accumulated. A small stained glass window in the rear wall depicted a sailing ship on the high seas. There were wrought iron candelabra and statues of saints and urns, but her full attention was captured by the carved stone ossuary where the bones of ancestors had found their final resting place—men, women and probably children, because the infant mortality rate was high in the mid-to late 1800s during the yellow fever epidemic.

She clenched her fingers to keep from trembling. "Did your family lose anyone in Hurricane Katrina?"

"We were lucky," he said. "Our only loss was property and belongings."

"It's hot in here."

"When the sun beats down, it's like an oven. You won't be in here for long." He took a step toward the door. "I will leave this open a small crack. If you see Jessop coming toward you or have any cause for alarm, give a shove and twist the key in the lock."

When he stepped through the door, her heart leaped. Her panic returned full force. She didn't want to be in here alone. She struggled to hang on to her dignity. No reason to be scared—this was only stone, marble, stained glass and… bones.

The door closed, but not all the way. A pencil-thin sliver of light cut through the darkness. She pressed her face against the ancient door and peered into the cemetery, where she could see Rafe leaning against the front fender of his SUV. The view was too narrow to be useful, but she could hear people outside talking and laughing. If she stayed here and remained unnoticed, she could eavesdrop on Rafe and Jessop.

How long? Every minute seemed like an hour. She tried to count and take slow, steady breaths, but the thick, muggy air clogged her lungs. Generations of pallbearers had entered this tomb to bid their final farewells. She wondered if Rafe would be buried here.

Stepping away from her listening place, she paced to the rear of the tomb and back again. *Damn, it's hot!* She peeled off her denim jacket, fanned her hand in front of her face and wiped away the sweat that had gathered at her hairline.

When she looked through the crack again, she saw Jessop saunter up to Rafe and shake his hand. The blond special agent matched Rafe in height, but Jessop was heavily muscled. He wore an untucked cotton shirt, snug across his well-developed chest and loose around his hips to hide his gun holster. He removed his sunglasses and asked, "Where is she?"

"Somewhere safe," Rafe said. "Never follow me again, my friend."

"Why not? What are you going to do?"

"A high-speed chase would not end well for you."

Jessop gave a short laugh. "I heard that you drove race cars in Florida."

"Perhaps," Rafe said. "Tell me about your connection with Charlotte."

"She's something else, isn't she? Don't let the

silver in her hair fool you. That is one hot, sexy lady."

Alyssa tried to suck air through the crack between the doors. The tomb seemed to be sapping her energy. Quietly, she dropped to her knees, conserving her strength. Rafe and Jessop talked about the logistics of getting in touch with Charlotte and bringing her to New Orleans. Davidoff was involved. Her aunt's stated goal, according to Jessop, was to appeal to her niece and get her to open up.

Their plan was ill conceived. Anyone who knew Alyssa would tell you that she was extremely guarded and slow to trust. Having her lying, cheating, supposed-to-be-dead aunt pop up after all these years would strengthen her resolve to stay silent—not that she had anything to say.

She heard Rafe ask, "Do you think Charlotte has something to do with the money?"

"Not Charlotte. If she had millions, she'd be living an extravagant lifestyle. Alyssa is a different story."

"As a federal agent, you'd be obliged to turn that money over to the government."

"I deserve a taste." Jessop cursed and then he laughed "Don't get me wrong—I don't expect to be taking a bath in hundred-dollar bills, but there ought to be a nice little payoff for me."

Rafe asked the most important question. "What do you and Davidoff want from Alyssa? What do you think she knows?"

Jessop glanced to the left and right as though looking for someone who might overhear. "I went over her files a dozen times and had the forensic accountants explain the details of the triple-entry system she and Horowitz used. Did she tell you about that?"

"Keep talking," Rafe said.

She appreciated that he wasn't giving anything away. Jessop didn't seem evil, but he was greedy. Under her breath, she murmured, "What does he think I know?"

"The reason everybody wants to talk to Alyssa," Jessop said, "is simple, and it doesn't have a damn thing to do with the accounting. Old man Horowitz wasn't smuggling, and his activity as a fence was minimal."

She was relieved to hear that her former boss wasn't a criminal. Her judgment about him had been accurate. He was a decent person.

"I'm losing patience," Rafe said. "Who was responsible for siphoning off the millions in cash?"

"You, more than anyone else, should be able to guess. You remember what happened in Florida when your undercover career was shot to hell by the Leone family. That's why I thought of you when Davidoff was looking for someone to be a bodyguard. You've got a reason to hate the Leones, and Frankie Leone—the warehouse foreman—was involved in the theft."

An involuntary gasp escaped her lips. She should have guessed. Frankie was involved in all the large transactions. He handled the inventory.

Rafe asked, "What does this have to do with Alyssa?"

"She held a dying man in her arms. With his last breath, he could have told her his secrets."

But he didn't. She struggled to suppress a sob. If Jessop overheard, he'd charge at the tomb and take her into custody. She pushed the door closed and twisted the key in the lock. Her only proof of innocence was her word. Why would anybody believe her? Through no fault of her own, she'd been condemned...might as well crawl into the ossuary and wait for her flesh to rot. Hopeless, she sank to the floor and wept.

Chapter Twelve

After confirming an appointment with Chance Gregory on his cell phone, Rafe watched Jessop walk down the aisle toward the wrought iron gates. The set of his shoulders and his athletic stride demonstrated the confidence befitting a federal agent. With his easy grin and the sunlight glinting in his blond hair, Jessop didn't appear to be a bad guy or a traitor, but Rafe could not consider him an ally. Jessop's motives were as tangled as the roots of the mangrove trees in the marshland. He liked his career as an agent but didn't mind getting dirty for the right payoff. He freely associated with Davidoff, a known criminal. Jessop didn't intend to hurt Alyssa but wouldn't hesitate to sacrifice her if she got in the way.

With these many contradictions and complications, nothing was certain. Rafe didn't know what to believe, but had to admit that Jessop was right about one thing: one of the reasons he'd agreed to work for Davidoff was a hint about the possible connection with the Leone family. Until Alyssa told her story about Frankie's murder, Rafe hadn't known how entwined she was with the family. He'd spent nearly a year working undercover with them and had never heard her name or any mention of the pawnshop in Chicago. His investigation had fallen apart, and he'd left too many questions unanswered. His time in Florida had ended in tragedy.

The Leones were not a topic he wanted to discuss with Alyssa, but he couldn't gracefully sidestep the issue. She'd been eavesdropping on his conversation with Jessop, and she'd demand an explanation, even if the story made him look bad.

As soon as Jessop was out of sight, Rafe climbed the marble stairs of the Fournier tomb. He kept his movements casual, trying not to betray his tension to other people who were walking in the cemetery. He tugged at the door handle. Locked! At some point during his conversation with Jessop, Alyssa had closed the door. Something must have spooked her. He called to her, "You can open up now, *cher*. He's gone."

He didn't hear a sound, not a peep. If he'd been the one sealed up in that cold, dank space, he would have gone mad. Alyssa was stronger, but she'd undergone a number of difficult situations in the past days, both physically and emotionally. Had she fainted? Was something wrong with her? His grip tightened on the handle, and he yanked hard. The old wood strained and jiggled but the door remained locked. He should have kept the key.

"Alyssa." He spoke into the place where the two doors met, hoping his voice would reach her. "You must unlock this door."

Logically, he knew she wasn't hurt. The time she'd spent in the monument was less than twenty minutes, not long enough to suffocate. The oxygen level was high enough to keep the votive candles lit. She was alone in the tomb. Nothing could harm her. Still, an unreasonable fear churned in his gut. He'd seen how nervous she was before he left her inside. Unmindful of the other people parading in the cemetery, he drew back his fist and hammered against the wood…once, twice, three times.

When he heard the sound of the metal key scratching against the lock, relief trickled through him. Silently, he assured himself again that she was all right. The door opened. He rushed inside and found her sitting with her bare legs sprawled out in front of her. Sweat glistened on her chest above her T-shirt. Her complexion had gone pale. Gasping, she said,

"Frankie didn't say a word...just died. I tried to stanch the blood but couldn't help him."

"Don't worry, *cher*." She looked so miserable that he would have given the entire seven point six million bucks to make her feel better. He lifted her in his arms, carried her into the sunlight and sat her on the stairs. "Everything is going to be all right."

"Don't you understand?" Her green-eyed gaze searched his face. "I have nothing to tell Jessop or any of the others. I don't know what happened to the money, but they don't believe me. And they're going to keep coming after me until..."

"I won't let them hurt you." Rafe took the key and returned to the darkened tomb to lock up from the outside.

"You can't stop them," she said. "They think I'm holding out on them. But when they find out that I really didn't hear a dying declaration from Frankie Leone, I'm no use to them."

If these treasure hunters had been reasonable, he might have convinced them to leave her alone. But greed had transformed them into frenzied gators chasing swamp rats and gulping them down in one bite. If they questioned Alyssa and didn't learn anything new about the missing money, they'd demand revenge. And she would pay the price.

"We need a plan," he said. "First step is to get away from here. Can you walk to the car?"

She staggered to her feet, aimed a determined gaze at his SUV and lurched forward. "I'll make it. Crank up the air conditioner full blast."

BEFORE HE DROVE down the aisle toward the exit gates, Rafe glanced into the back seat, where Alyssa was curled up on the floor so no one could see her. Her T-shirt clung to her body, and her shoulders hunched. She looked like hell, and he didn't want to add to her woes, which meant he didn't tell her that if anybody had been observing them in the cemetery, her location had already been pinpointed. Plus, Jessop wasn't an idiot. While they talked in the cemetery, the fed had cast many suspicious glances toward the tomb and repeatedly asked about her whereabouts. He could have figured out that Rafe and Alyssa were together.

That conclusion was undeniable and unfortunate. She was not safe.

Their escape from those who pursued them would not be based on clever disguises or secret hideouts. In this moment, they needed to go on the run. Their survival depended on his detailed knowledge of the city where he grew up, and he was confident that his skill in navigating the detours and shortcuts and roundabouts would be enough. He could outsmart a bloodhound on the scent. Not to mention that his driving skills were exceptional.

After they left the cemetery, her disembodied voice rose from the back seat. "Where are we headed?"

"We're going to the home of my friend and colleague, Chance Gregory. He's a cyber genius. We can get more data from him in an hour than from talking to Jessop for days."

"And where does he live?"

"You'll be surprised, *cher*."

Though Chance lived with his mama, he wasn't a typical computer nerd who buried himself in a grungy basement and existed on a diet of cheese puffs and beer. He might best be described as an old-fashioned gentleman of the South. His family owned one of the classic antebellum plantations along the Mississippi River Road that ran between New Orleans and Baton Rouge.

"Speaking of surprises," she said as she popped up between the seats, "is there something you want to tell me about Frankie Leone?"

"How much did you overhear?"

"Jessop said you took the job offer from Davidoff because there might be a connection with the Leone family in Florida. How do you know them?"

"Through an extended undercover assignment," he said, fighting through his reluctance to talk about that time in his life. "Before I moved back to New Orleans, I was investigating their smuggling operation in Florida. Though I was close to several people in the family, I never met Frankie and knew nothing of his operation in Chicago."

"Is that true? You really didn't know the identity of the victim in my crime?"

"All I knew was that you witnessed a murder." Her skepticism frustrated him. Would she never trust him? "If I heard mention, the victim was referred to as a warehouse foreman."

"Did you enjoy undercover work?"

When she peeked around the edge of his seat and stared at his profile, he noticed that her wan complexion had returned to normal. "Covert operations can be *très difficile*, especially when they are long-term."

"You have to be a good liar to pull it off."

"I suppose." He tried to brush off the unfortunate direction of her questions. "It was my job."

"You were deceiving people for months at a time."

He stopped for a light and turned his head to confront her directly. They were close, almost nose to nose, and he was momentarily captivated by the facets of silver and hazel in her green eyes. He inhaled and regained his composure. "There are times for lies and times for truth. I know the difference, *cher*. I'm being straight with you. Ask me anything."

"I will." She pulled back. "In Florida, what was your cover story?"

"I passed myself off as a race-car driver."

His driving skills were nowhere near professional level, but he talked a good game. The Leone family accepted him as an eccentric Frenchman who had participated in several Grand Prix races in Europe. He recalled that ruse while he drove through New Orleans making unpredictable turns and dodging anyone who might be trying to follow his SUV.

Alyssa jostled backward as he slammed on the brake. "Watch it! You're not on a racetrack now."

"Put on your seat belt, *cher*."

He heard her rearranging herself behind him before she said, "Tell me more about the Leone family. What kind of smuggling did they do?"

"They owned a legitimate trucking company, but their trucks were sometimes filled with stolen merchandise, mostly appliances or electronics. They were considered small-time operators and too unimportant for the FBI to investigate."

"I don't understand. Why did you go undercover?"

"Information suggested that the Leones were expanding their operation into the smuggling of illegal weapons and possible drug trafficking." He guided the SUV through a sharp left turn. His goal was to evade pursuit until he left the city limits. At his friend's home, he could borrow another vehicle.

"Did Jessop give you any new information?"

"Currently, the FBI believes that Frankie was responsible for the missing millions."

"That's crazy!" Her disbelief exploded from the back seat. "I can't give you an accounting down to the penny, but I guarantee that the pawnshop wasn't making so much money that Mr. Horowitz wouldn't notice if seven point six million dollars went missing."

"Think about it, *cher.* Frankie's thieving was spread out for a very long time, all the way back to ten years ago when he was dating your aunt. And Horowitz was known to keep high-ticket items in his warehouse. Davidoff used to store some of his vehicles there, including a vintage Rolls-Royce that was worth close to three hundred thou."

For several long minutes, they were both silent. He imagined that she was remembering the many expensive objects that were housed in the Chicago warehouse. The locked safe was large enough for her to walk inside, and it must have held precious objects of great value. Over the years, it wouldn't have been difficult for Frankie to remove these artworks, jewelry, antiques and furs—especially since some of these items had been stolen in the first place.

"I can't believe it," she murmured. "Mr. Horowitz was careful with his inventory. He would have noticed."

"Not if Frankie was clever enough to replace the real objects with forgeries. He was in charge of the warehouse and had complete access. There would be no record of the pickup because he used trucks from his family's business to ship out the merchandise."

"If that's true, Frankie was a whole lot smarter than I gave him credit for. What was his mistake? What got him killed?"

"Greed." That seemed to be the underlying motive for everything that had happened. "Frankie deviated from the plan. Instead of funneling the merchandise to his family, he set up his own operation in Chicago."

"A double cross," she said. "He was stealing from the warehouse and double-crossing his family while building his private fortune. Then Ray McGill shot him. How does he fit into this picture?"

"The FBI has known for a long time about the connections between the McGill family and the Leones. They're criminals but still business-men."

While she repeated and reviewed the twists and turns of Frankie's scheme, he checked his rearview mirror. After several blocks, he determined that they weren't being followed, and he set a course for the Mississippi River Road.

Under different circumstances, he would have enjoyed taking Alyssa on this trip, giving her a view of the more refined aspects of life in New Orleans. Not everything was about jazz and Mardi Gras and parades in the streets. The city was one of the oldest settlements in the country. Traditions ran deep.

"About the Leones," she said. "Jessop said something about how your assignment with them destroyed your career. I want to hear the whole story."

He'd hoped to avoid this painful memory. "My mistakes aren't relevant."

"I want to know the truth. You say that you aren't lying, but hiding the details is deliberately misleading." She exhaled a powerful sigh that he heard in the front seat. "I want to trust you, Rafe."

And he wanted the same thing. "After several months with the family, I earned a place in their organization as a getaway driver."

"For bank robberies?"

"Never a bank. But there were meetings when it was necessary to make a swift escape. I kept the FBI informed, and they acted appropriately. Sometimes there were arrests. Other times, there were not. By the time my investigation was drawing to an end, I had become friendly with several in the family, including a young mom named Deedee who was routinely abused by her husband."

He remembered that slender creature with her long black hair and soulful eyes. Deedee looked older than her twenty-two years, except when she was playing with her two toddlers. That tiny glimpse of her happiness had touched his heart. One day, she'd confided in him, revealing that she was pregnant again and terrified of how angry her husband would be.

"My assignment had been a bust," he admitted to Alyssa. "I hadn't uncovered gun smuggling or drugs. The Leone family appeared to be small-time crooks and nothing more. I wanted my time with them to mean something."

"You tried to help Deedee," she said.

"I referred her to people who could protect her from her husband and help her establish a new life for herself and her children. I should have stayed with her, shouldn't have left her alone with strangers."

"I understand," Alyssa said. "You thought you were doing the right thing."

He should have known better. After the time he'd spent in Florida, he should have realized that Deedee's loyalty to the family and to her husband was more important than her personal safety. She went back to her abuser.

As soon as Rafe heard, he'd raced to their house. Too late.

"He killed her."

Chapter Thirteen

Sitting in the back of the SUV with her seat belt fastened, Alyssa couldn't see Rafe's face, but she heard the intense pain in his voice, and she knew that he blamed himself for Deedee's death. "What happened to the children?"

"They were placed with a good family, and the arrangement seems to be working out. The foster parents are planning to adopt the boys. I send payments for their care."

"It sounds like you're doing the best you can to help out."

"Money is not enough. These babies lost their mama. I'll make sure that no one—especially not their father, who is incarcerated—will hurt them again." He jiggled his shoulders as if he could shake off the anger. "That's my story, *cher*. Have you heard enough?"

Though she appreciated how hard it was for him to talk about Deedee's murder, she had other questions. "Jessop said the Leones messed up your career. Is that true? Did you get fired?"

"The opposite," he said. "The FBI was very willing to sweep Deedee's murder under the rug and call it a case of domestic violence. They hoped I could continue undercover. But no, I couldn't stay in Florida. I had to come home to New Orleans and figure out what was the right course for the rest of my life."

"And you came up with being a private investigator?"

"For now, it works. I'm my own boss, I don't have to take orders from anyone else and I can use my training."

"Your special skills? Like beating up thugs in skeleton masks and escaping from a second-story warehouse window and tearing up the streets with your evasive driving? An interesting collection of talents, but I've got to admit that you're good at what you do."

"Merci."

"I'm guessing there's something else driving you. You're not a pirate—you're a hero. I think you enjoy helping people like me, doing the right thing."

Again, he shrugged. "I like being able to choose which jobs to take and which to turn down."

"Why did you choose me?"

He pursed his lips and scowled. "Now and then, everybody makes a mistake."

His little joke diverted their conversation from uncomfortable topics like honor and nobility. She was glad that he didn't take himself too seriously. Not everything that happened was about him. She hoped that Rafe didn't think Deedee's murder was his fault. If anything happened to her, he wasn't to blame.

He was a good man. But she didn't dare tell him so—not yet, anyway. Trusting him would be easy but risky. He might disappoint her. "Thanks for telling me about Deedee."

"You shared details about Frankie Leone's murder. Turnabout is fair."

"It's good to know that you're dedicated to your job—keeping me safe from the idiots who think I'm the key to finding their fortune."

"Was there any doubt?"

Outside her window, the landscape had changed. They'd left the city behind and were driving north on a divided four-lane road into a more sparsely populated area. "Where are we?"

"River Road." He pointed to the right. "Over that ridge is the levee, and beyond that is the Mississippi. This drive was once famous for the many plantation-style mansions."

The buildings they passed were far more mundane—gas stations, odd shops and tired-looking

houses. Beyond the oaks, poplars and shrubs at
the roadside, she glimpsed a ramshackle two-
story structure with faded gray columns across
the front. It looked like the great-great-grand-
mom to Tara. "What happened to the plantations? Were they destroyed in the hurricane?"

"Nothing so dramatic. The mansions grew
old, required too much upkeep and were abandoned." At an intersection, he turned left and
drove through a very small town. "We'll stick
to back roads so no one can track my SUV."

"There's not much traffic," she pointed out.
"We'd see anybody who follows us."

"I'm concerned about drones."

In spite of her massive paranoia, she realized
that his knowledge of surveillance and tracking
techniques was superior to hers. When she'd
planned her getaway routes, she'd tried to consider every detail and contingency, but drones
had never crossed her mind. If she hadn't been
with Rafe, Alyssa doubted she would have survived the first assault by Woodbridge and his
skeleton crew.

They drove along a two-lane asphalt road that
curved through an overgrown area of streams,
reeds, shrubs and ancient oak trees with long,
twisted limbs that reached toward them like
the grasping, gnarled fingers of witches. Span-
ish moss draped from their boughs. This close

to the river, humidity thickened the air. "Your computer genius lives around here?"

"Chance Gregory is one of my oldest friends. We went to the same prep school. Across that field, that's his family's place."

In the distance, she spotted a two-story white mansion with pillars that reached from the veranda to the shingled roof. The carpet of grass on the hill leading to the magnificent entrance was neatly trimmed with autumn flowers planted in tidy beds. Two monstrous oak trees loomed behind the structure like sentries, and a weeping willow in the front completed the picture.

"I'm impressed," she said. "Keep in mind that I lived in Savannah, and I know what Greek revival–style architecture looks like."

"The best part about this place is the horse barn in the back. Chance raises thoroughbred race horses and Arabians."

She wished that she'd been wearing a more appropriate outfit. Her khaki shorts and sweat-soaked T-shirt seemed far too casual. Clothing shouldn't matter. People in Chicago didn't seem to pay too much attention, but Alyssa's mom had taught her about proper attire for a lady. *If you dress for the occasion, people take you seriously.*

"I must look a mess." She found a mirror in

her backpack, slapped on a dab of blush and arranged her hair. "Can we explain to your friend that I was locked in a tomb for what seemed like hours?"

Rafe drove the SUV up the curved driveway leading to the Gregory mansion and circled around to the back. Outside a long garage, a slender man in jeans and a denim shirt stood waiting. He directed Rafe to pull into the last parking bay. Inside the garage, the SUV was completely hidden. Because of drones?

She slipped into her jean jacket, still musty from the tomb, climbed from the back seat and latched onto Rafe's arm. He leaned down and whispered, "No need to worry, *cher*. You're beautiful."

Outside the garage, Chance greeted her with a kiss on both cheeks that somehow didn't seem phony. His hair was light brown, his eyes were blue and he smelled like lemons.

After Rafe introduced her, Chance said, "I didn't believe it, but my old partner in crime was right as rain. You are Scarlett O'Hara come to life and ready to rule the bayou."

She opened her mouth and closed it again. "I don't know what to say."

"Come inside and have something to eat. Mama and Auntie are at church, but I have leftover jambalaya and corn bread from last night."

Rafe joined them. He was taller than Chance and broader across the shoulders. Rafe's features were more rugged, especially his chiseled cheekbones and the dent in his chin, but there was a similarity between the two friends. Maybe it was the cool assurance behind their eyes. Maybe it was the way they both had kissed her when they met for the first time. She couldn't say why, but she was a little bit fascinated by Chance.

She gave him a nod and said, "I'd love to taste your mama's jambalaya."

"Don't get too deep into hospitality," Rafe warned. "That goes for both of you. We've got work to do."

"I'm way ahead of you." Chance led them through the back door into the mansion. "I've already been digging into the business of Diamond Jim Davidoff and the Leone family. Which do you want first?"

"Davidoff," Rafe said.

They entered a well-equipped country kitchen that was big enough to prepare a sit-down banquet for a couple hundred people. It was obvious that Chance knew his way around food preparation, and he talked while he reheated the spicy, redolent rice and andouille dish, warmed the corn bread and threw together a light salad.

"Viktor Davidoff goes by the name Davis

James or Diamond Jim, but his real name is a
poorly kept secret. As far as I can tell, he has no
family connections in the Chicago area, but he
has links with the Russian mob in New York."

"Are you sure there's no family?" Rafe asked.

Chance set a plate of corn bread on the coun-
tertop, planted his fists on his hips and glared.
"What's wrong with you, partner? You know
better than to question my research. I'm never
wrong."

Rafe scoffed. "Never say never."

"I'm curious," she said. "Why do you call
Rafe your partner? Did you work together?"

"It's slang," Chance explained. "In Cajun, a
pal is called partner."

"My pal Chance speaks crisp, clear English."
Rafe gave him a nudge. "The true pronuncia-
tion is 'podnah.'"

Chance completed the thought. "Rafe is my
podnah, and you are his boo."

For the second time today, someone had as-
sumed that she and Rafe were in a relationship.
Was this a conspiracy? "I'm nobody's boo."

He took a pitcher of lemonade from the fridge
and handed it to her. "Please take this into the
dining room."

When she stepped through the kitchen doorway into a gracious room with high ceilings and
tall windows, a sense of contentment settled

over her. She recalled similar homes in Savannah when she was a child. This was how life was meant to be—civilized and genteel. The generous proportions of the dining room were balanced by a china cabinet, a linen cupboard and a long oak table with seating for five on each side. Two polished brass chandeliers over the table were unlit. There was no need for artificial light with all those windows.

At the end of the table, Chance had set three places with woven mats, plates, bowls and tall crystal glasses. The dusty-pink napkins complemented the centerpiece of orange and yellow blooms—mums, dahlias and carnations. She was beginning to understand what Rafe meant when he described his "podnah" as a gentleman. Chance appreciated the finer things in life.

After the two pals brought the rest of the food to the table, she relaxed even more. The jambalaya was delicious with spicy bites of andouille. The cold lemonade refreshed her throat and washed away the memory of being locked in the tomb. For the first time since the *Día de los Muertos* parade, she began to believe that everything might turn out all right.

"Can I get you anything else?" Chance asked.

"It's all good," she said, "really good."

"I hate to introduce an unfortunate topic," he said, "but I need to warn you, both of you. Mr.

Davidoff—or Davis or Diamond Jim—is a very careful man. He dresses with precision, keeps his goatee trimmed and his jewelry polished. He hired a brilliant bookkeeper who can legally account for every penny even though Davidoff is most likely engaged in fraud, tax evasion and smuggling. Likewise, his attorneys are meticulous. Frankie Leone's murder caused a disruption in Davidoff's business."

"What kind of disruption?" Rafe asked.

"As near as I can figure, Davidoff had taken possession of three vintage cars that were worth over two hundred and fifty thousand dollars each. One went missing." Chance rolled his eyes. "The very thought of that Lamborghini V12 makes my mouth water."

A glance at Rafe told her that he was also captivated by that mental image. She would never understand why men loved pieces of machinery. Cars had never aroused her. As a teenager in Chicago, she preferred taking the bus or the L train so she didn't have to mess with parking. "Did Frankie steal the car?"

"It seems that he did," Chance said. "After years and years of carefully removing objects from the warehouse, Frankie Leone overstepped."

Her good mood began to crumble around the edges. "How do you know all this?"

"It took some serious hacking." He reached into his shirt pocket, pulled out a thumb drive and handed it over to Rafe. "The details are here, but I think you'll both agree with my conclusions. In the end, Davidoff was working with the Leone family in Florida, who were not real happy with their cousin Frankie double-crossing them for years."

"To the tune of seven point six million dollars," Rafe said.

"How did somebody like Frankie get away with this?" She sipped her lemonade. "I mean, this was a sophisticated operation using forgeries. He must have developed a network of criminal connections to fence the property. He couldn't just walk up to some person on the street and offer to sell them a Lamborghini. How did he pull it off?"

"By hiding in plain sight," Chance said. "Nobody paid much attention to Frankie Leone the warehouse foreman. He didn't live a flashy lifestyle, didn't buy fancy clothes or women. There was only one time when he got in trouble. That was ten years ago."

"When Aunt Charlotte got involved."

"She could be in trouble."

"In danger?" Alyssa didn't want to care, but she did. Charlotte was the only family she had left in the world.

Chance made direct eye contact. "Your auntie isn't in as much trouble as you are. Rafe tells me that you're a woman who makes plans. I would suggest that you exercise that ability. You need to find a way to leave town and lie low."

Tomorrow, after she retrieved the necessary items from her safe-deposit box, she'd get away from New Orleans. "Is there anything I can do for Charlotte? She's working with Agent Jessop of the FBI, you know. How much danger is she really in?"

"I'll put it to you this way," Chance said. "The only way Frankie survived ten years ago was to put all the blame on her. That was why she had to fake her death. They were all after her—the Leones, other smugglers, Horowitz and everybody else."

Not her old boss! Of all the people she knew, he was the one she trusted the most. He'd helped her through the terrible time after her mom's death and had been nothing but kind. If anyone could rescue her from this mess, it was him. "Are you sure Mr. Horowitz was after my aunt?"

"I am," Chance said. "And I'm seldom wrong."

Chapter Fourteen

Cruising back to New Orleans on the Mississippi River Road in a Mercedes C63 sedan, Rafe almost believed his undercover identity as a Grand Prix driver was true. The ride was sheer perfection. Chance had insisted that they take his twin-turbo V-8 sedan to evade surveillance by drone, camera or any person who had the license plate for Rafe's SUV. It hadn't taken much convincing for Rafe to agree to the trade.

His first choice would have been Chance's racy red two-seater Porsche. But Alyssa pointed out that the car attracted too much attention. The sleek lines of the metallic-gray Mercedes didn't look all that much different from other vehicles on the road. But it was—oh yes, it was. Driving this high-performance vehicle was as satisfying as harnessing the power of a rocket ship and taking off for the moon.

"You're going over seventy," Alyssa chided

from the passenger seat. "We don't want to get pulled over."

A typical police car could never catch this powerful vehicle, which, according to Chance, went from zero to eighty in less than four seconds, but she was correct. They wanted to escape notice.

Reluctantly, he eased up on the accelerator. "I didn't realize I was breaking the speed limit. The suspension system is so good that I don't feel any bumps on the road."

"Very comfortable," she said.

He fondled the steering wheel. *"Magnifique."*

For a moment, they rode in comfortable silence. Their bellies were full, the ride was smooth and a bond was growing between them. He wanted this feeling to continue and deepen. Life would be easier if he aimed the nose of the Mercedes toward the west—away from Florida or Chicago—and kept driving until he found a safe place where he could sit with Alyssa and hold her without fear of attack.

"I like your podnah," she said. "Chance is different from any other computer nerd I've ever met."

"He's a mite crazy, but he's never let me down."

"He was right when he said I need to come up with a more detailed plan."

"First, you've got to make a big decision," he said. "Will you stay in New Orleans, or will you go on the lam?"

"On the lam? That sounds so…criminal. I guess I never thought about staying here. The plan was to run, and I made tons of arrangements from transportation and escape routes to fake identification. I never owned a lot of assets, but I inherited a bunch of cash when Mom died and got a hefty insurance payoff from Charlotte's death." She caught her lower lip in her teeth as she paused and considered. "If I know she's alive, is it fraud to keep the money? I should probably pay back the insurance company."

"You're going off track," he said. "Stay or go?"

"That brings up another set of questions. If I decide to stay, should I contact law enforcement? The FBI and the marshals are out, so that leaves NOPD."

"I know some of the local cops—people who can be trusted."

"Even when there are millions on the line?"

The temptation to betray her would be tempting, even for the most morally upright officer. He didn't feel good about leaving her in the care of a system that had already revealed a rotten core. "Putting yourself in police custody means you give up on further investigation. You know how it works, *cher*. You aren't entitled to information or follow-up. The detectives ask questions, and you answer."

"And no one gets arrested." Her fingers curled into a fist, and she pounded on her thigh, emphasizing each word. "Just. Like. Before."

During his years in the FBI, he'd been on the other side and knew how hard it was to pry details from witnesses. "It's not always so bad."

"It's been three years since I went into WitSec, and nothing is solved. Turn myself in? No, thanks, I've already taken that route."

"You know the alternative," he said. "We do our own investigation."

Her mouth spread in a wide smile. "That sounds right to me."

He found her confidence somewhat disturbing. Their chances of outsmarting federal and local law enforcement weren't good. Not to mention Davidoff, the McGill family and the Leones. A lot of very motivated people were trying to solve this puzzle. What made her think she'd succeed when they all had failed? He had to wonder if she knew some detail that she hadn't revealed.

"That's your decision," he said.

"It is."

"Where do we start?"

"With Charlotte," she said firmly. "I don't owe that woman squat, but she's the only family I have left, and I'm concerned about her survival. Chance thinks she's in danger. At the very least, we need to warn her."

Contacting Charlotte wouldn't hurt their investigation. "She might give us leads on the missing millions. After all, she was Frankie's lover."

"She can tell us how he pulled it off. I know he wasn't smart enough. She must have helped him set it up." Enthusiasm rippled through her voice. "Maybe she can give us the names of her connections and we can follow up."

Rafe doubted that Charlotte had many secrets left untold. She'd probably shared the names of any contacts with Jessop and the FBI, which meant that Davidoff had the same information. Still, talking to her was worth a shot. "You have her phone number. Give her a call."

Sheepishly, she said, "I already tried. I called her from Chance's house. She didn't answer, so I sent a text."

He couldn't see her eyes behind her rhinestone sunglasses, but he could tell she was both excited and tense by the way she fidgeted and chewed her lower lip. "I wish I could tell you not to worry about Charlotte. She could be in danger. Keep in mind that she's not without resources."

"What does that mean?"

"The woman returned from the dead. She's been in hiding for ten years while appearing in public as a lounge singer. I'm not sure if she's on your side or is working for somebody else. Your aunt Charlotte is a wild card."

Alyssa bobbed her head in agreement. "She'd adore Chance. The gracious living, the charm and the manners are her favorite things. I wish we could have seen his thoroughbreds."

"We'll visit him again. I've got no choice about that. My podnah is going to want his Mercedes. In the meantime, I suggest you contact Sheila Marie. If anyone can find Charlotte, she can." He took his phone from his pocket and handed it to her. "I took a photo at the church. Send the picture of Charlotte and mention that she's a singer."

Approaching the city, he needed to be on high alert, watching for people who were looking for them. Rafe kept one eye on the road and the other on Alyssa as she put through the call to Sheila Marie. His phone was his lifeline containing information about the security at the house and his many contacts. He couldn't help worrying that she might scroll through and uncover something he didn't want her to see. No matter how many times he told himself to trust her, he couldn't set all his suspicions aside.

Unlike Jessop and Woodbridge, Rafe believed her when she said that the dying man hadn't told her any secrets. Her outrage when she'd confronted her aunt was genuine, which meant that Alyssa wasn't working a con with Charlotte. His misgivings came when he considered her skill as an accountant and her insider knowledge of how the pawnshop worked. Her familiarity with the place was second only to Horowitz's. Every time his name was mentioned, she bristled. Her feelings for her old boss went beyond the typical employee relationship.

Alyssa ended her call and turned to him. "Sheila Marie says hi. Her exact words were, 'Where y'at?' And I told her that you were happily driving a fancy Mercedes. She wants to take a turn behind the steering wheel."

"Not going to happen."

"She said that she'd look for Charlotte and let us know if she found her." Alyssa held the phone toward him. "You have a text from Davidoff. I didn't read it, but I think he wants you to call him."

That was exactly the kind of information he didn't want her to know. Davidoff was a topic he'd rather not explore in great detail. He pocketed the phone. "I'll check in with him later. Right now, we're headed back to the safe house."

Instead of the evasive driving he'd used when he knew Jessop and maybe Woodbridge were after them, he concentrated on obeying the traffic rules and blending in with all the lesser automobiles. Like a beautiful woman, the Mercedes didn't need to flaunt her superiority. Any fool who took a second look would recognize her value.

On a Sunday afternoon after a wild parade the night before, New Orleans felt lazy and comfortable. In the French Quarter, tourists meandered on the streets, carrying daiquiris and Bloody Marys in plastic cups. Music emanated from every little jazz club.

"I want to get started investigating," she said. "What can we do tonight?"

He would have liked to spend the evening getting to know her better. Not from what she told him or what he'd learned on the internet. He wanted to know her in a physical sense. When he thought about the natural heat from her body, his gut tightened. He could tell in a glance that she was in good shape, but he wanted to caress her arms and legs, to feel her strength. His arms ached to hold her. So far, he'd done a real good job of keeping his distance. They'd developed a certain level of trust, and he hoped she would let down the barriers that guarded her heart.

He cleared his throat. "We can review the case. I know you've been questioned by dozens of professionals, but never by me."

"Do you think you can figure out something they missed?"

"Can't hurt to try."

"Fine." She spread her hands wide with her palms up. "Ask me anything. I'm an open book."

"Let's start by talking about Horowitz, *cher*."

The book slammed shut.

After all her demands that he tell her the whole truth, Alyssa was holding back. She had a secret, and her former boss was part of it.

AS SOON AS they arrived at the safe house, Alyssa told Rafe she was tired and wanted to take a nap. He could hardly blame her. Though today hadn't been physically demanding, she'd been hit with one shock after another, from meeting up with her supposedly dead aunt to being locked in a tomb. Any reasonable person would need a rest.

In the room that was supposed to be a mirror image of her bedroom at home, she kicked off her shoes, peeled off her jacket and stretched out on top of the chenille bedspread that was a duplicate of the one she'd purchased several months ago. She liked being surrounded by her things—which really weren't hers, but looked like them. In spite of her tension, she relaxed. Soft afternoon light from the windows shone on her bedside table and the Toulouse-Lautrec poster on the wall at the foot of the bed.

Figuring out a plan for what they should do after the visit to the bank was going to take focus. A different concern was foremost in her mind. While they'd been driving here, she'd managed to evade Rafe's questions about Mr. Horowitz, but she wasn't sure how long she could keep from telling him the truth.

Her former boss had disappeared after the murder, and everybody—feds and criminals alike—had a stake in finding him. Horowitz was the most probable person to know where the money had gone. After all, he owned the pawnshop and handled all the merchandise. His awareness of the inventory was encyclopedic. How could millions disappear without his express knowledge and consent?

Over and over, she told herself that Max Horowitz was an honest man. She trusted him, believed in him and knew he wouldn't do anything illegal. Before he skipped town, he'd told her that she wasn't alone. If she needed him, he would be there. Then he gave her a phone number, which she memorized. If she called the secret number, he would know that she needed his help. But she could only call in the very worst-case scenario—worse than being pursued by Woodbridge or the feds, worse than being on Diamond Jim's enemies list and worse than meeting up with Charlotte. The threat had to be literally life or death. Even then, she wasn't sure she could bring herself to betray Max Horowitz.

When she closed her eyes, she remembered the pleasantly musty smell of his sweater-vests and jackets. When he chuckled, his mustache twitched. He was only a few inches taller than she was, but he was surprisingly strong—an ability that served him well when he had to move heavy merchandise. While he worked, he liked to hum, mostly old Beatles tunes.

Thinking of him soothed her nerves. Her eyelids gently opened, and she was pleased to see the pale yellow she'd chosen to paint the walls. She inhaled the vanilla and cinnamon scent from her homemade potpourri. She didn't mind being here. Maybe Davidoff had been on to something when he'd arranged for a dupli-cate bedroom.

Rafe tapped on the door. "Are you decent?"

"I'm dressed."

He stepped inside, carrying a tray with two tall glasses of iced tea and a small bag of Zapp's spicy potato chips. "The tea is sweet," he said.

"That's how I like it." Iced tea in Chicago wasn't typically sweetened, but her mom had clung to her southern habits, and Alyssa was fond of the sugary flavor. "Thanks, Rafe, but I have to ask. Are you buttering me up?"

"You insult me." He placed the tray on the dresser, handed her a glass of the tea and took the other for himself. Then he tossed the bag toward her. "Chips?"

"There's nothing yummier than the Cajun gator flavor." She tore open the bag. A sip of cold tea and a crisp bite of spicy heat made a perfect combination. "How did you know that I love these chips?"

"Remember, *cher*, I've been watching you for two and a half weeks."

The idea of having him stalk her had been insulting when he first told her, but now his constant observation felt like a compliment. "What else did you learn about me?"

"You like to go running in the morning and don't mind working up a sweat. The gym doesn't hold your attention as well, not even the swimming."

"Yeah, you're right. I never got into the lap swim. And I don't like diving into cold water."

"I guessed as much."

When she realized that he'd been watching her in the pool, she wondered what he thought of her sleek one-piece swimsuit with the high-cut legs. She didn't want to seem conceited, but she was proud of being fit. She nibbled another chip. "What about you? Do you work out?"

"But of course."

Their conversation was beginning to sound like pickup lines at a bar, which was crazy, because they ought to be past that kind of chitchat. "You know a lot more about me than I know about you. I don't have to tell you my astrological sign, which is Aries, by the way."

"I know."

"And you know that I'm terrible at crafts, except for making stinky potpourri. I've already told you about the places I've lived and the important things that have happened in my life. It's like we're jumping into the middle of a friendship instead of poking around the edges."

He cocked an eyebrow. "I think you'll like where we're headed."

Her pulse began to accelerate. He'd kissed her within moments of introducing himself at the parade, but that had been a polite kiss on the forehead. If she was reading his intention correctly, Alyssa knew she was in for the real thing. "You're in the driver's seat, Rafe. Where do you want to take me?"

Chapter Fifteen

Alyssa had lobbed the ball into his court. There was nothing to do but sit back and wait for Rafe to make the next move. Another kiss would be good—a serious, sexy kiss that was a whole lot more than a polite greeting. She made bold eye contact, staring deeply into the splintered facets of his gray eyes. Then she lost her nerve and looked away. Her breath tangled in her throat. Her heart beat faster.

Every passing second felt like an hour, and she mentally prepped herself for the possibility that he'd reject her advance even though she felt their attraction when they touched, heard it in the way he called her *cher* and saw his appreciative glances. He liked her looks, and she knew it. But other stuff stood in the way, like his need to protect her, the temptation of the missing millions, which he had to be thinking about, and—most importantly—trust.

She hadn't been completely honest with him. Did he know it? Did he sense it?

He reached toward her and took the glass of iced tea from her hand. Without a word, he carried both glasses to the dresser and set them down where they wouldn't spill. When he came back to the bed and sat close to her, her pulse was racing faster than a drumroll.

Gently, he took her hand and said, "I want you to trust me."

Had he been reading her mind? Were they on the same page? *Please don't ask about Horowitz, please.* She felt her lips quiver. "Same here."

"There's something I need to tell you, *cher.* This might be difficult to hear."

Was he married? He hadn't mentioned a wife or a girlfriend. Neither Sheila Marie nor Chance had brought up the topic. But that might be Rafe's big secret. She snatched her hand away from him. Darkly, she said, "There's another woman."

The expression of surprise on his face would have been comical if she hadn't been so ticked off. He rattled off a stream of French that was liberally punctuated by denial before he switched to English. "I am not a perfect man. For years, I made my living undercover, telling lies. But I have never betrayed a woman I love. If I were married or involved with another, I would have told you from the start. No, *ma ché-rie*, there is no one else."

"Then what is this big, fat secret and why will it be hard for me to hear?"

"I spoke to Davidoff on the phone."

Five minutes ago, those words would have sounded a disturbing note of fear in her belly, but not anymore. Compared to the idea that Rafe might be hiding a secret wife, the mention of Davidoff seemed trivial. She had to wonder if her priorities were askew. "What's up with Diamond Jim?"

"The photo of you that we took in the cemetery lit a fire under him. He thought you looked frightened, and he wants to meet."

"With me?" She flapped her hands, waving away the request. "That's not going to happen. Davidoff is a criminal."

"I'm not so sure that he wants to harm you."

"Because he hired you as a bodyguard? Ha! That's no reason." She scooted away from him on the bed, pulling her knees up and pressing her back against the headboard. "Did you forget about Jessop? He's after the money, and he is most definitely in Davidoff's pocket."

"And possibly Charlotte, as well."

Davidoff was the ringmaster, snapping his whip and directing the clowns, tigers and acrobats in this crazy circus. She didn't want to believe that Rafe was part of the show, but he'd done Davidoff's bidding. His orders had been to follow her and to decorate this room to match her own.

Moments ago, she'd thought the similarity was comforting. Was she falling under Davidoff's spell? "I don't understand what kind of game he's playing, but I want no part of it."

"He told me a secret that makes sense of everything," Rafe said. "I promised not to tell, but it's unfair to withhold this information. You need to know everything before you make your decision."

The anticipation was nearly unbearable. "Spill it."

"Viktor Davidoff claims to be your father."

She was stunned. All her life she'd fantasized about the identity of her father, praying he was a prince and fearing that he was a monster. Her mom told her that he'd spent time with her when she was an infant. He'd held her and sang lullabies, but she couldn't remember the words. There were no photos, no cards, not a single note from him. She had a hazy memory of her fourth birthday party, when he gave her the music box, and she seemed to recall him telling her that she was his favorite girl and he would always take care of her.

If Davidoff was that man, he hadn't lived up to the promise. "Why wouldn't he tell me?"

"Think about it," Rafe said. "He didn't want to put you and your mom in danger from his enemies. When he first moved to Chicago, there were clues that he was escaping from the Russian mob in New York."

"I heard those rumors but I never paid much attention." She shook her head. "He hasn't been my father for twenty-seven years. Why now?"

"I don't know."

In the back of her mind, a tiny spark of hope ignited. Was it possible? Having a father would change her core identity. If he truly was her father, Davidoff couldn't be such a terrible person. Her mom never would have fallen in love with him. Maybe if she got to know him, she could accept him. And then she remembered…

As quickly as hope had been born, the light was extinguished. She glanced at the bedside table, where the lamp with the fringed shade stood beside the potpourri. "Where's my music box?"

He went to the dresser and opened the top drawer. "After you threw the box at the wall, I figured you didn't want it anymore."

"Give the thing to me." As soon as she held the box in her hand, she knew it was a fake. The wood wasn't as smooth as the original, and the patina was lighter. "My father gave me a music box when I turned four. Not this box but another. Before I went to sleep, I'd rub the wood against my cheek. And I'd open the lid and listen to the music—my music, 'Lara's Theme' from *Dr. Zhivago*."

She flipped open the lid and heard "Twinkle, Twinkle Little Star."

"Davidoff never mentioned the tune," Rafe said. "Your real father wouldn't have allowed me to make that mistake. He would have given specific instructions."

The trick Davidoff had tried to pull on her was beyond cruel. He had played on the emotional needs of a fatherless child who had also lost her mom. She had no family. Asking Charlotte to be part of her life was like trying to bond with a feral cat. "He's truly a bastard."

"His claim was strange but somehow made sense," Rafe said. "He hired me to protect you, which is what a father would do. When he talked about you, he seemed sincerely concerned about your well-being. And Lara is a Russian name, short for Larissa. Davidoff might have chosen that name for his daughter. Lara Davidoff?"

"Yuck! Mom picked my name because she thought it sounded pretty. And it's not like Davidoff is the only Russian I know. Lots of people come from that part of the world, like

Mr. Horowitz. His first name, Max, is short for Maksim. And one of the McGill brothers married a Russian woman who blames me for testifying against her husband." Alyssa's temperature was rising, and the initial hurt she felt was turning to rage. She rose up on her knees. "Why are we talking about this? I'm not Davidoff's daughter. There's no way I'll agree to meet with him."

"I'll find a way to get rid of him."

Still angry, she climbed off the bed and stalked across the bedroom to the dresser, where she grabbed her iced tea and took a long drink. The cool liquid failed to quench the fire burning in her belly. "Why would he make up that particular lie? What did he hope to gain?"

"Your trust."

She steamed across the bedroom and back to the bed. After she placed her glass on the bedside table next to the Zapp's bag, she hopped onto the chenille spread. Rafe watched her warily as though she were an exotic creature in a zoo.

"I'll never trust Davidoff," she said.

"Is there anyone, *cher*? Anyone whom you trust?"

Though she could have run down a long list of associates and friends who watered her plants when she wasn't home, that wasn't really what he was asking. Rafe wanted to know if she trusted him—a fair question. He'd proven his loyalty many times over. Now that he'd told her about Davidoff's grand scheme to pose as her absentee father, she had the feeling that all his cards had been played. He had nothing left to hide.

There were dozens of other questions she could ask, teasing out the details of how he'd learned the colors in her bedroom and if he'd followed her home after a party at work when one of the servers tried to kiss her. She could ask about his time undercover and his other FBI assignments. But trust was a feeling, not an accounting.

She believed in him and didn't need proof. "I trust you, Rafe."

He lowered his arms and crossed the small bedroom in a few quick strides. First, he went to the two windows near the bed and pulled down the blinds to block the late-afternoon sunlight. The room dimmed, and she turned on her bedside lamp with the fringed shade. The glow was soft, soothing and intimate.

The first thing he took off was his shoulder holster, which he hung over the wooden chair by the tiny desk. Then he returned to the opposite side of her bed and held out his hand as though asking her to dance. She was so ready for this tango. When she grasped his outstretched fingers, he pulled her toward him. Rising up on her knees again, she closed the space between them.

His arm encircled her, and he gently rested his hand at the small of her back. She hadn't felt her bruises for most of the day, but his nearness heightened her sensitivity. There was a twinge. Her nerves were humming. The surface of her skin prickled.

He leaned close and whispered, "I trust you, *cher.*"

She didn't deserve his trust. She was still holding on to a secret. But she wasn't about to switch gears and talk about Mr. Horowitz. Not right now. She was ready for this special dance with him and had been expecting it from the moment he'd introduced himself as a pirate at the parade. She glided the back of her hand down his cheek and held his jaw. Her thumb traced his lower lip and explored the dimple in his chin.

Her head tilted back, ready to receive the kiss that she knew was coming. His mouth joined hers with a firm but gentle pressure that elevated her desire into the stratosphere. She suspected he'd be a skillful lover. The man was French, after all. If this kiss was any indication, she wouldn't be disappointed.

At just the right instant, the tip of his tongue

tasted her lips and pushed inside to probe the interior of her mouth. Excitement pulsed through her. She wanted him to be closer, wanted to feel the weight of his body atop hers. Leaning backward, she pulled him off balance onto the bed.

Her maneuver wasn't exactly graceful, and they ended up in a tangle of limbs. When they got their bodies sorted out, she was on her back. She wrapped her legs around his hips and reveled in the full-body contact. Her need was maybe a little too aggressive, because he slowed the pace and separated from her.

Breathing hard and wanting more, she gazed up at him. She was so mesmerized by his smoldering, sexy eyes that she hardly noticed when he started unbuttoning his white shirt. He was using only one hand, and it was taking too long.

"I'll help." Her fingers trembled as she unfastened the buttons. "Is there some word for what we're doing in French? Some romantic phrase?"

"We call this sex," he said.

"Oh good, we're on the same page."

With the buttons out of the way, she opened his shirt. Though she'd seen him bare-chested in the morning before breakfast, being this close was better. His skin was darkly tanned, and the hair across his pecs and washboard abs made an intriguing pattern. She drew a line down the center of his chest with her index finger, pausing to swirl the hair and admiring the tight muscularity from his collarbone to the waistband of his trousers.

"Your turn," he said, interrupting her quest.

Within seconds, he'd removed her T-shirt and slipped off her bra. "Speedy," she commented. "I didn't even feel you unfasten the hooks. That must take years of practice."

"I like looking at you," he said. "You are *magnifique*."

He used that word a lot, and she liked being in the same category as the Mercedes. Before she could make a smart comment, he lowered his head and nuzzled her breasts, paying particular attention to her nipples.

Her back arched, and she closed her eyes. A low moan slipped through her lips and hung in the air. There was no time for comments or chatter. She abandoned herself to the pleasure he coaxed from her body with his light caresses and kisses that covered her torso. She wanted more.

Wordless, they tore off the rest of their clothing. She pulled him against her with all the strength she could muster. She wanted him inside her. Clinging to the last thread of conscious control, she felt truly alive. *More, more, more!* She didn't want him to stop, not now, not ever.

Vaguely aware of what was happening, she

realized that he'd put on a condom. Where did he get it? Did he keep a supply in the bedside table? She didn't care but was glad that her bodyguard had taken the need for protection seriously.

He rose above her on the bed and spread her thighs. Shivering and shaking, nearly weeping, she endured gentle nips, licks and kisses that descended from her breasts to her belly to her groin. His fingers teased and manipulated, raising her level of arousal to amazing heights.

He covered her with his body. His heat flowed through her. His heartbeat synchronized with hers. Finally, he penetrated her. Her gasps became moans as he drove into her, harder and harder until she completely lost control and exploded like fireworks into a million sparkling pieces.

After the first glittering bursts, she lay back and enjoyed a rumbling earthquake of sensation that shook her from head to toe. It took a while for her breathing to return to normal and for her racing pulse to resume a sensible pace. Then another aftershock hit. She whimpered like a kitten.

He stroked her hair off her forehead. "Are you all right?"

"Fine, I'm fine. I'm fine." Another tremor rippled through her. "How about you?"

He spoke to her in French. Though she didn't know the language, she caught a few words about champagne and roses. "Translation?"

"It's poetry, *cher*. I'm comparing your mouth to a rosebud and the taste of your breasts to the sparkle of champagne."

She liked the musical French version better. "Whatever you're saying, thanks."

He lay back against his pillow and stared up at the ceiling. "At a time such as this, I hate to bring up unpleasant subjects, but we have an investigation that we might pursue tonight. Chance gave me a thumb drive with raw data from the accounts of the pawnshop and the inventory. I've glanced at the information. It means nothing to me, but you might be able to translate the numbers into leads."

She allowed another aftershock to chase through her body. Getting her feet solidly back on the ground was going to take a few minutes. "I can compare Chance's data with a copy of the accounts and inventory from the last few months before Frankie was killed."

"You have these accounts?"

She nodded. "There's a thumb drive in my safe-deposit box. I turned over the original to the feds, but it seemed prudent to keep a copy. I've studied the list but didn't notice anything out of the ordinary."

"Tomorrow," he said, "we will compare this paperwork."

"And tonight, what will we do tonight?"

He traced his finger across her lips, leaned close and whispered in her ear. "I want to thoroughly investigate every inch of your body."

She liked that plan.

Chapter Sixteen

They stayed in the bedroom until the sun set and the streets were dark. Rafe could have spent many more hours lying beside her—naked, happy and fulfilled. He laced his fingers with hers and brought her small, slender hand to his lips. She was lovely, delicate. Her apprehension was gone, erased by a sexual compatibility that surprised him. He hadn't expected them to be so good together.

Yes, she lacked experience. But she was graceful, enthusiastic and energetic. Alyssa held nothing back. She made him feel like he'd invented sex.

Cradled in the crook of his arm, she gave him a contented smile worthy of an otherworldly angel, then she reached up and booped the tip of his nose. "I'm hungry. What should we do for dinner?"

"I wish we could go out," he said. "New Orleans has incredible restaurants, but we don't want to risk the exposure."

"I guess that means we've got to cook."

He tossed aside the spread, rose from the bed and stretched his arms over his head. "Come with me to the kitchen."

"Whoa, podnah. You're not planning to make dinner in the nude, are you?"

He glanced over his shoulder. "There's no reason for either of us to wear clothes."

"Oh yeah, I can think of a few negatives, like not wanting to get grease spatters on the delicate parts of my anatomy. And we're still in danger. We should be prepared to run at a moment's notice."

He liked her intelligence and her wit. "You always think ahead."

"Which is why I'm still alive," she said. "Meet you in the kitchen."

He charged down the hallway to his bedroom, where he put on a pair of jeans, a black polo shirt and running shoes. He hadn't been planning to go out tonight, but it didn't hurt to get all the way dressed and ready to run. He even fastened his holster to his belt. Earlier tonight, he'd brushed his teeth but hadn't shaved. His stubble was heavier than usual. A shower would have felt good…a shower with Alyssa would be better.

In the kitchen, he took a couple of rib eyes from the fridge and threw brown rice in the cooker. On the table, he set up the laptop for Alyssa and loaded the thumb drive Chance had given him. After he made a marinade for the steaks, he gathered ingredients for a tomato and cucumber salad.

Alyssa seemed to be taking her time getting to the kitchen. When she finally strolled through the door, dressed in a coral blouse and shorts, he noticed her damp hair. He kissed her forehead and inhaled the peachy fragrance of her shampoo. "You took a shower," he said. "I would have been happy to join you."

"Not surprised." She stroked his jawline. "It's okay with me if you don't shave. I kind of like the unkempt look."

He knew that he couldn't spend every minute of every day fondling her and he should set boundaries. But he couldn't resist another kiss. He yanked her tightly against him and realized that she hadn't bothered to put on her bra. Though tempted to sweep everything off the table and make love right here, he put on the brakes.

"Did I tell you how beautiful you are?"

She looked uncomfortable. "You don't have to compliment me every minute just because we, you know, did it."

"Not an obligation, it's my pleasure. But you are correct. Unfortunately, we have other concerns. Voilà! Here is the computer."

She sat in front of the screen, tapped a key and smiled when a row of numbers appeared. "Is this the data from Chance?"

"Ready and waiting for you."

While she scrolled through the pages, he finished preparing their meal. Though he wasn't a great cook, the arrangement pleased him. He liked taking care of her.

Apparently, she'd reached a stopping point, because she stepped away from the computer, helped him load the plates and placed them on either end of the table while he poured the chilled Chardonnay. "I can't believe Chance got access to all this info. Not only are there ledgers and receipts, but he found personal correspondence and FBI stats. He even tapped into a psychologist report about me. Guess what the guy said."

He sipped his wine and sliced off a juicy bite of rib eye. "Tell me."

"He claimed that I had abandonment issues because my father ran off when I was a little kid. Also, he called me fearful and tense and suggested that I might have some kind of anxiety disorder. Well, of course I was upset. A man died a violent death in my arms, and I'd been whisked into WitSec. Still, he should have noticed that I'm resilient, strong and brave."

"And sexy," he added.

"That goes without saying."

She dug into her food with her typical enthusiasm. Their conversation was replaced by a series of appreciative moans, which were not unlike the sounds she made in the bedroom. Finally, she paused to take a drink of her Chardonnay.

"Here's what I'm wondering," she said. "Obviously, some of Chance's data was uncovered through illegal hacking. Is there any database he can't get into?"

"I've never known him to be stumped."

"That's disturbing." She gestured to the computer and the kitchen and the house at large. "We're protected by your surveillance and computer firewalls, but there has to be someone—a hacker who is as talented and smart as Chance—who could break through and find us."

"I built this surveillance system using my FBI training and state-of-the-art equipment. Plus, you'll be happy to note that Chance added his very own special mojo to anticipate every kind of attack."

"Chance did that?"

"That's got to make you feel better. My podnah used his superior technology to make this place nearly impregnable and invisible."

"Any fortress can be broken into," she said, "because of human error."

"And so, we can't make mistakes."

He wanted to believe that was possible, but Rafe knew better than to count on perfection. Sooner or later, they might get careless. After they finished eating and cleaned up the dishes, they went into the small front room and had a cup of chamomile tea while they made tentative plans for the following day. Another glass of wine would have been nice, but that was an easy mistake to avoid. He needed to stay alert. In the morning, their first stop would be at her bank, where they would pick up her thumb drive and compare her data with the information Chance had provided.

"Then we should get my second car," she said. "The key is in the safe-deposit box."

"We could have gotten the car at any time, *cher*. I might not actually know how to win a Grand Prix race, but I know how cars work. I could have hot-wired the ignition."

"I'll keep that in mind in case things go south at the bank. There are tons of things in the trunk of that car—a computer, clothes, shoes, cash and credit cards in a different identity."

He hadn't forgotten how resourceful she was.

"We can use all those things. With Davidoff coming to New Orleans, the city is even more dangerous than before. Moving somewhere else might be wise."

She sipped her tea and licked her lips. "Before we go, I want to figure out where the missing millions are hiding. Finding the money is the only way I'll be truly safe."

She seemed to be ignoring the threat from the families of the men who went to jail because of her testimony, but he didn't remind her. One horror story at a time was enough. Besides, her odds for survival were greatly improved because he would be at her side, constantly protecting her and ever vigilant.

His cell phone rang. The caller ID showed the call was from Sheila Marie. Rafe suppressed a groan, recognizing that she'd be calling with new information and they'd have to leave their cozy nest. He put the call on speaker.

After a quick hello, Sheila Marie said, "I done found Missy Charlotte with the silver hair. She's at the Corner Oak Tavern on Bourbon Street."

He heard a bluesy saxophone wailing in the background. "Is she singing with the band?"

"Not a bit of it. This lady is slumped down and drinking hard. She looks sad."

"Keep an eye on her," he said. "If she leaves the Oak, let me know."

"Got it, boss man."

"Wait for me outside. I'll be there in a minute. Is there a place you can take Alyssa where she'll be safe?"

"No prob. I got a dozen hideouts."

He believed her one hundred percent. Sheila Marie knew the city better than anyone. "*Merci beaucoup.* See you in ten minutes."

Alyssa was on her feet. "Do I need a disguise?"

"Keep it simple."

He watched her dash down the hallway to her bedroom. Bringing her along might be a mistake, but he had no choice. She couldn't stay here by herself.

In minutes, she joined him in the Mercedes. Instead of the fancy pink outfit, her disguise was to go minimal: no makeup and slicked-back hair tucked under a black baseball cap with "Mardi Gras" written across the front in letters of purple, green and gold. From a distance, she'd be unrecognizable. He had no disguise, only a blue windbreaker over his black shirt. They didn't have time for anything more complicated.

As she buckled her seat belt, she said, "Thank you."

"For what, *cher*?"

"Meeting with Charlotte. I shouldn't worry

about her, but I can't help it. We need to get her to safety, which means far away from New Orleans."

His reasons for seeing her aunt weren't completely altruistic. She'd been in on Frankie's smuggling scheme from the start and might have helpful information. She had contacts in the criminal world. Someone considered her useful enough to pay her bills for ten years. Rafe welcomed the opportunity to question her without having her sympathetic niece standing by.

He approached the location of the Corner Oak and spotted Sheila Marie standing under a streetlamp. On a Sunday night, there were still tourists milling around but not a crowd. He pulled up to the curb.

His favorite confidential informant climbed into the back seat. With her long dreads, an embroidered turquoise blouse and a long paisley skirt with swirls of red, green and yellow, she was an explosion of color. The first thing she did when she got into the Mercedes was stroke her fingers—polished half red and half yellow—across the upholstery.

"Leather," she said. "Man, you oughta keep this fine ride."

"It belongs to Chance."

"Oh yeah, I like that boy, even if he does live on a plantation." She flicked her hand toward the windshield. "Go straight, turn on Bourbon Street and then left. We be paying a visit to Jolene's voodoo shop."

He knew the place. "Alyssa, wait for me there."

"Take your time," Sheila Marie said. "Alyssa should have a reading. Jolene can see the future. Dat's good, yeah?"

"Sure," she said. "I went to a psychic in Chicago after my mom died. She didn't tell me anything I didn't know, but she made me feel better."

Dropping her off in a voodoo shop felt like a bad idea, but meeting with Charlotte had the earmarks of a trap. He wished he could take Alyssa home where they'd be alone and safe. But there were unavoidable hurdles they had to jump to reach the truth.

Before she left the car, she leaned across and kissed him on the lips. "Take good care of Aunt Charlotte."

"I intend to." He couldn't wait to get that woman out of town.

In moments, he'd returned to the Corner Oak Tavern, parked illegally and entered the dimly lit jazz club. The four-piece band followed their own jam, shifting from drums to piano to guitar and sax. A woman with bright red lipstick swayed and murmured a sad song about being left by the only man she'd ever loved.

Charlotte should have been on stage; she had a better voice and more presence. But she sat by herself at a small round table in the audience. Her two-tone rum cocktail looked like she'd barely taken a sip. When he pulled out a chair and sat, she shot him a sidelong glance, and he knew this would not be a friendly interview.

"Ten years ago," he said, keeping his voice low, "you were in love with Frankie Leone. The two of you ran a smuggling scam using the pawnshop warehouse."

"Who sent you? Was it Jessop? Or was it my snippy little niece?"

"Someone else could be looking for you."

Her head snapped up, and she stared. Now he had her attention. She spoke in a trembling whisper. "What are you talking about?"

Though he was tempted to tell her that Davidoff was on his way to New Orleans, Rafe didn't want to give away too much information without getting something in return. He gestured toward the stage. "I expected to see you singing."

"Not my gig."

"It could be. If you unleashed that voice of yours, people would clamor to hear more."

"That's a nice fairy tale, but talent doesn't get you far."

He added bitterness to the long list of her

negative traits that included lying, cheating and stealing. "You know the business."

"I've got more talent in my pinkie toe than that singer has in her whole body, but singing doesn't pay my bills. That's why I'm sitting here, waiting for Jessop. He's half an hour late." She looked down into her cocktail and muttered, "He knows where I'm staying. I don't know why he wanted to meet here."

Rafe had a pretty good idea why Jessop would stage a meeting outside her room. "He wanted you out of the way so he could search your place."

She sipped the drink and set it down on the table. "You're not as dumb as you look."

"Neither are you," he said. "You didn't leave anything for Jessop to find. Being on the run for ten years means you know how to think ahead. Here's the irony. Your niece is the same way. She wanted me to come here to warn you."

Charlotte didn't bother to pretend that she was dumb or innocent. "What's the warning?"

"You need to give me something first. I'm pretty sure that Frankie didn't come up with the logistics of a lucrative smuggling operation, double-crossing his criminal family by using forgeries and fences. Frankie Leone just wasn't that smart."

"He wasn't, bless his heart. My Frankie was

funny, sexy and devoted to me. But he was no genius. I came up with the basic plan, and I'd be happy to jot down the names of my contacts. Not that those names will do you any good."

"Why not?"

"It was ten years ago. My list is dated."

Unfortunately, she was right. "Anything you can tell me might help."

"Use your brain, sonny boy. There's only one name you need to know, only one person who can explain everything. That person is Max Horowitz. He knew everything that went on in his pawnshop and warehouse. I wouldn't be surprised to learn that he partnered up with Frankie after I left town."

Similar thoughts had occurred to Rafe. Siphoning off millions of dollars could be part of a scam to avoid paying taxes. Horowitz had something to hide. Why else would he skip town after the murder? He pushed back his chair. "Take me to your hotel room."

"What's in it for me?"

"Davidoff is on his way to New Orleans, and you need protection. Jessop can help and so can I."

The arrival of Davidoff was good motivation for her to move fast. She gathered up her huge purse—probably filled with the necessities of her life—and they left the Oak.

On the street, he didn't waste the effort to engage in conversation. She was Jessop's problem.

For Alyssa's sake, Rafe would keep her aunt safe until she could be taken into protective custody. As they walked through the crowd, he scanned for threatening people who mingled with the cheerful tourists and bar hoppers. He spotted a pickpocket and a sinister drunk who yelled at anyone who crossed his path.

Her hotel was small but charming, located only a block off the main route. Instead of being trapped in the rickety old elevator, he climbed the staircase to her second-floor room. On the landing, he motioned to her. "Which room?"

She pointed to a door that stood ajar. Before going forward, Rafe pulled his weapon from the holster on his hip and held it ready. Charlotte stayed behind him, moving silently. Her attitude told him that this wasn't the first time she'd walked into danger.

Entering her room, he flipped on the overhead light. Everywhere was chaos—overturned chairs, drawers pulled from the dresser, clothing scattered on the floor. The mattress had been pulled off the box spring. In the tiled bathroom, he found Jessop, lying on the tiled floor in a puddle of blood. A head wound matted his blond hair.

Rafe squatted beside him and felt for a pulse. Jessop turned his head and groaned. He wasn't dead.

Chapter Seventeen

"Death comes close. He carries a sword. He rides the white horse." Jolene, the owner of Dragon's Blood Voodoo Emporium, held the tarot card toward Alyssa and jiggled the edges so the skeletal death figure looked like he was dancing. "He comes for you."

Sheila Marie reached over and patted Alyssa's hand. "Doncha worry, hon. Dat card is not so bad."

"Really? Are you telling me that death isn't a bummer?"

"Death don't always mean being buried in the cemetery—could be an end of things, like a bad habit."

"Truth," Jolene said. "Many smokers come to me."

Her gestures were quick, darting, almost birdlike. Her skinny arms waved emphatically when she talked, clanking her many bracelets and sending her necklaces twirling. She fluttered energetically in the back room of her shop, where a huge mural of dancing skeletons and a fire-breathing dragon decorated the walls. The shelves were lined with candles and jars filled with mysterious substances. Incense tainted the air and mingled with the scent of something bubbling in a pot on a hot plate. Alyssa hoped the stew was chicken.

She didn't really believe in voodoo or magic, but she found the practice interesting. Besides, getting a reading from Jolene was a good alternative to thinking about what was going on with Rafe and Charlotte. "Can you really use magic to get people to quit smoking?"

"If they believe in dragon's blood," Jolene said, "I can cure them."

"Where do you find dragon's blood?"

"Special formula. It comes from plants and trees." She held a small vial containing a crimson liquid. "Very precious. I use dragon's blood to make the gris-gris I sell in my shop."

"A gris-gris is a lucky amulet, right?"

"And so much more. My gris-gris wards off evil and turns away zombies."

She'd been in New Orleans long enough to understand that voodoo wasn't always about ugly little dolls to stick pins into and rituals to cast dark spells. Most of the magic involved love potions or ritual enchantments to bring fame and fortune. "Can I buy a gris-gris necklace from you? I need all the protection I can get."

"First, we talk of your future." Jolene touched the bill of Alyssa's baseball cap. "Take this off."

She removed the cap. "Now what?"

"Sit, my child."

Alyssa sank into the patterned cushions of a low rattan chair. Glancing at her phone, she checked the time. Rafe had been gone for eighteen minutes. She estimated eight to ten minutes to get to the Corner Oak Tavern and back here. That meant he'd been talking to her aunt for about eight minutes. Would he bring her here? Could he convince Charlotte that she was in danger?

Jolene combed her fingers through Alyssa's hair. "Clear your mind," she said. "Stop your worrying. Forget your woes."

Not necessarily good advice. Alyssa tended to suppress her negative emotions. A therapist had told her she needed to deal with all these issues: abandonment by her father, her mom's early death by hit-and-run, witnessing a murder and the whole WitSec thing. *No, thanks.* She'd rather do it the voodoo way. "Forget my woes."

Perching like a colorful canary, Jolene took a seat on the opposite side of a small round table draped in woven kente cloth from Ghana. She motioned for Sheila Marie to join them. "Alyssa, place your hands on the table, palms down."

She tilted her vial of dragon blood and allowed a drop to fall on the back of Alyssa's hand. While she murmured incomprehensible syllables, Jolene smeared the red liquid in a jagged pattern. She put on a good show. Alyssa's only other experiences with fortune tellers hadn't been half so dramatic.

"In your future," Jolene said, "there is a man."

Sheila Marie cackled. "Tall, dark and handsome, I betcha."

"Not this man. He is not tall. A nice smile..." She rubbed her upper lip. "And he has a mustache. A kind man and strong, he has many secrets."

She had to be talking about Max Horowitz. Ever since Alyssa learned that Davidoff was coming to town, she'd been thinking that it was time to make the emergency call to her former boss. "Will he help me?"

"He would do anything for you. He would die for you."

That wasn't what she wanted to hear. Dragging Mr. Horowitz into danger was the last thing she wanted. "If I call him, what will happen?"

"I cannot say." She leaned back from the table, distancing herself.

"That's not fair," Alyssa said. "What kind of fortune teller are you? I need answers."

"I'm not a carnival act." Quickly, Jolene leaped to her feet, ready to take flight. "I am a seer. I connect with the future and the past. I can advise you, my child, but there are too many variables to make an accurate prediction."

"Advise me. Should I contact this man?"

"The decision is yours," she said archly. "It's not my job to make you happy."

"Back it up," Sheila Marie said. "You got to tell her about the French man with the powerful mojo. He is important."

"When it comes to him, she doesn't need my advice," Jolene said. "They are already bonded, hand to hand and heart to heart."

Alyssa liked the way that sounded. She peered at the painted bamboo curtain that separated this small room from the outer store. Any minute, Rafe should be here.

In the meantime, she bought a gris-gris amulet that was marked with genuine dragon's blood and found a quiet corner to make her phone call to Mr. Horowitz. She punched the number she had memorized into her phone. After three rings, a mechanical voice answered and repeated the number back to her. She selected her words carefully, not wanting to give too much away.

"You told me to call if I needed your help, and I do. Everyone thinks I know where the millions are hidden, and I might have a clue if I can compare inventory with my accounting. At least, I'll know what was stolen. I miss you. All I want is for this to be over. Life used to be safe and calm, and I want that life back."

She stopped herself before she launched into a nostalgic memory of the Christmases he'd spent with her and her mom or the spring days when they strolled along the lakefront. This wasn't the time for sweet, soft memories. She needed to be strong.

"Charlotte came back from the dead," she said. "Seeing her makes me think of Mom."

Her comment was too personal. If anyone other than Mr. Horowitz was listening, they'd know she was the caller. "Anyway, please get in touch with me. I'm in New Orleans. Oh yeah, and I met a guy. You'd like him. 'Bye for now."

Before she put her phone away, she checked the time. Rafe had been gone for forty-two minutes. A lot of bad mojo could happen in that amount of time.

RAFE PERFORMED BASIC first aid on Jessop. The bleeding was minimal, and there were no deep lacerations from gunshot or knife wounds. Jessop had been beaten, and his head wound was beyond Rafe's rudimentary skills. He shouted over his shoulder at Charlotte, "Call 911."

"I can't. This is my damn room. The cops will think I did this."

He doubted there was anybody who'd suspect her of pistol-whipping a physically fit, well-trained federal agent. Charlotte was tall but didn't have the muscles to inflict this level of damage. "Just make the call."

"Can we move him out of my room?"

"He's unconscious and in bad shape. By moving him, we might make his injuries worse." Why was he even talking to her? He took his phone from his pocket and tapped in the numbers.

"Rafe, no. You don't understand. I can't go to jail."

"We'll wait for the ambulance, and I'll get you out of here."

"But the room is in my name."

An alias, he thought. After ten years on the run, Charlotte knew better than to use a name that could be traced. When the 911 dispatcher answered, he gave the important information. "We have a 10-999, officer down, immediate assistance requested. Send a bus to this address, second floor."

Instead of staying on the line as instructed by

the dispatcher, he disconnected and looked over at Charlotte. "Bring me a pillow and a blanket."

"Why?"

"To prevent shock." Jessop was breathing steadily and groaning." Rafe leaned close and spoke with urgency. "Who did this to you? Give me a name."

Still, Jessop didn't open his eyes. If anything, he squeezed them shut, blocking out the over-head light in the bathroom. When he tried to move, it was apparent that his right arm had been injured. Likely, his shoulder was sepa-rated—an injury that Rafe could fix if Jessop moved into the right position. He decided to wait for the paramedics.

Jessop's eyelids fluttered as though he was struggling to regain consciousness, trying to wake up and name his attackers. Rafe encour-aged him. "Tell me, *mon ami*. Who hurt you?"

There had to be at least two of them, maybe more. Rafe took the pillow from Charlotte and used it to elevate Jessop's head. Though he didn't wake up, Jessop responded with a gasp. His mouth opened. A thin trickle of blood spilled from the corner.

Rafe tried to reconstruct what had happened in this room. Jessop wasn't the sort of man who came up with elaborate conspiracies; his actions would be straightforward. He had arranged to get Charlotte out of the way, drinking at a blues club. While she was gone, he went to her room. But why? What was he looking for? She must have evidence in her possession. He remembered that Jessop had a connection with Davidoff and might have been doing his bidding.

The thugs must have been waiting in the room to ambush him. If they'd interrupted Jessop midsearch, he would have pulled his weapon, and it didn't look like he'd had time to get off a shot. His holster was empty, and there was no smell of gunpowder in the air. The men who attacked were cowards and definitely not geniuses. Leaving a witness alive wasn't a smart move.

Charlotte peeked over his shoulder. "Is he going to be okay?"

This was the first time she'd showed concern. "With a head injury, his condition is unpredictable."

"He's a nice man. I hope he recovers."

From outside, he heard the scream of an approaching ambulance. "Do you know who attacked him? Can you take a guess?"

"You mentioned Davidoff," she said.

"Why would he come after Jessop? Does he want something from you, Charlotte?"

In an angry huff, she stamped away from the

bathroom, returned in a shot and snapped at him. "Can't you just take my word? It was Davidoff."

"You're a liar and a scam artist. I wouldn't take your word for the time of day if you showed me a clock." The ambulance was louder. "You need my help, Charlotte."

"Get me out of New Orleans, and I'll tell you what Davidoff wants."

Not a great deal, but he had very little choice. The longer he stayed at this crime scene, the longer Alyssa was unprotected. "Listen to me, Charlotte. When the paramedics get here, stay out of the way. They'll have to use the staircase to move Jessop. The elevator is too narrow."

"Should we take the elevator to the ground floor?"

"Too obvious," he said. "The bastards who attacked Jessop are probably watching."

"What should I do?"

"Grab your necessary stuff. We've got to run."

He wiped his hand on a towel before sending a similar text to Alyssa. Be ready to go.

Moments later, they heard the EMTs coming up the staircase, dragging their equipment and complaining with every step. While Charlotte disappeared into a closet, Rafe directed them to the bathroom. "This man is a federal agent. Check his wallet."

"You should stick around, pal. The police are going to have questions."

"You got here fast, *merci*."

"Pas de quoi." The paramedic grinned. "It's our job."

Rafe stepped out of the way while they worked on Jessop. He was lucky that the ambulance arrived before the police A call of "officer down" usually brought an aggressive response. He heard their sirens approaching.

Charlotte came toward him. She had used her few minutes alone to prepare for flight, changing from a light dress to black slacks, black jacket and sneakers for running. She had a small backpack on her shoulders. He was glad to be wearing a dark-colored windbreaker to cover the blood. They would blend into the darkness, and they needed every advantage to evade the local police and the people who had attacked Jessop. "You need to do as I say," he told her.

"Absolutely."

Her quick agreement was something of a surprise. Alyssa never would have accepted his leadership without a fight. Maybe her aunt had something to teach her after all.

Without exchanging a word, they exited her hotel room and rushed to the elevator. Instead of going down, he hit the "up" button, taking them to the fourth floor where they exited into an empty hallway. So far, so good. He motioned for Charlotte to follow and crept down the hall to a door at the end of the hall. He jiggled the handle, played with the lock. The door opened onto a fire escape.

Rafe went first. On the metal fire escape, he ducked and peeked through the bars at the chaos in the street below. Two ambulances and four police cars blocked traffic. A crowd of watchers gathered on the sidewalk, chatting and drinking.

He scanned until he saw a man who stood alone and didn't seem to be observing the police action. Instead, he stared at the building, watching. He tilted his head and looked up.

Though Rafe had only seem him once before from a distance, he recognized Woodbridge.

Chapter Eighteen

Nervous, Alyssa paced on the wood floor in the front shop at Dragon's Blood Voodoo Emporium. Moments ago, she'd gotten a text from Rafe, warning her to be on the lookout for Woodbridge and his buddies. Her thumb rubbed the leather of the gris-gris amulet that hung from her neck, and she prayed that Rafe was unharmed. Sending him to meet with her aunt might have been a mistake, but she couldn't ignore the signs of danger that pointed at Charlotte like daggers.

Sitting outside the door by the front window, Sheila Marie kept watch for Rafe and the luxurious Mercedes. The night shadows didn't dim her vivid clothing. If anything, she seemed more colorful. She held a wooden drum between her knees and tapped a rhythm on the tautly stretched head. More than once, she pointed tourists toward another shop and told them to come back in fifteen minutes. Jolene had asked her to keep people away until they knew Rafe was all right. Though the fortune teller couldn't really see the future, she didn't want to take a chance that a tourist would be injured in her shop.

Jolene poked her head around the bamboo curtain and flashed a too-bright, toothy grin that hinted at mischief. "May I introduce you to my dearest companion?"

Reluctantly, Alyssa said, "Okay."

With her arms spread wide and her hands gesturing gracefully, Jolene stepped into the front of the shop and slowly turned in a circle so Alyssa had a chance to admire the companion she'd mentioned: an eight-foot-long, brown-and-black-patterned snake. Alyssa didn't have a problem with reptiles. One of her friends in Chicago was a stripper who used snakes in her act.

"Burmese python," Alyssa said. "May I touch her?"

"She would enjoy being touched. Dominique is my sacred serpent, a creature of great wisdom and magic."

Alyssa stroked the smooth skin, marveling at the muscularity of the snake as it coiled around Jolene's arm. "Are snakes important in voodoo?"

"I don't use Dominique as much as I could," she confided. "But she's very helpful when it comes to warding off bad people. Many fear the snake."

"A matter of taste."

Carrying her drum, Sheila Marie bustled through the front door and charged toward the back of the shop. "I saw the fine Mercedes. Rafe is almost here. He gonna come through the back door, like I told him. Go, Alyssa. Wait for him."

"Hide in the closet," Jolene said. "Don't come out until I give you the signal."

Alyssa wasn't bothered by the Burmese python, but she didn't know how Rafe would feel. "Do you have any of Dominique's friends stored in the closet?"

"There's a cage full of food. Rats."

"Okay."

She ducked behind the curtain but didn't rush to get into the closet with the rats. Instead, she peeked into the front of the shop, where Sheila Marie had settled down with her drum. Jolene went out the door, chanting and dancing with her snake. When she returned, a few tourists came with her. Within five minutes, others arrived. They must have been locals, because they were carrying their own drums and singing their own tunes.

Woodbridge stepped through the front door. She immediately recognized his hatchet jaw. As she pivoted toward the rear of the shop, she saw

Rafe enter. Charlotte was with him, but Alyssa barely noticed her aunt. Rafe was the center of her world.

She dashed across the room and leaped into his arms. He was here. He was safe. Everything would be all right. She wanted to indulge in a long, deep kiss, but now wasn't the time.

Though the drumming and dancing were loud, he kept his voice low. "What's all the noise from the front of the shop?"

"The voodoo dance of the sacred serpent." She grabbed his hand and pulled him toward the closet. "Jolene said to wait here. Aunt Charlotte, that means you, too."

Muttering under her breath, she followed them. "You two have really made a mess of things. I was doing just fine until I came to New Orleans."

Sadly, the feeling of disgust was mutual. Alyssa would like nothing better than to build a loving relationship with the only person left in her family, but Charlotte wasn't the happy, imaginative, loving aunt who'd played games with her when she was a child. This silver-haired woman with the beautiful voice was cold, bitter and deceptive.

"We didn't bring you here." Alyssa opened the door to the closet. "By the way, there's a cage full of rats in here. Don't scream unless you want to die."

"I'm too tough to scream. Why would I die? Who's after you now?"

She looked up at Rafe. "I saw Woodbridge come into the front of the shop."

He hustled them into the closet and pulled the door almost all the way closed. They could still hear the drumming and chanting. Jolene's voice was louder than the others'.

In a tuneless wail, she called out, "Death is coming, coming for us all. Feel his icy presence. Welcome him. The serpent will bring the truth."

A man gave a hoarse shout. "Get that thing away from me!"

"Death is very near to you."

"I mean it, lady. I'll kill that snake."

"And burn in the damnation fires for eternity." She let out a cry. "Look at him! People, look at his feet. He has blood on his shoes. Who did he kill?"

"Back off, voodoo bitch. I'm out of here."

In the closet, Alyssa looked up at Rafe. Just enough light leaked through the crack in the door for her to see the dimple on his chin. His head tilted down, and she knew he was looking at her. She asked, "Was Jolene talking to Woodbridge?"

"I wouldn't be surprised to find out that he has blood on his shoes."

"Who died?"

"Jessop was badly beaten. We called the paramedics, and I'm hoping he'll survive."

"And you suspect Woodbridge." In her mind, she'd placed Jessop into the bad-guy camp along with Davidoff and Charlotte. Still, it was possible that he was working for someone else. Double-crossing each other seemed to be standard procedure, which didn't explain the attack. "Why would Woodbridge take that kind of risk? Why assault a fed?"

"Don't be stupid," Charlotte growled. "They all want the money. Until you tell them where it is or how to get it, they'll keep coming after you."

"I don't know anything, but that doesn't mean I'm stupid."

"Call it naive," Charlotte said. "Would you please change places with me? I don't want to be back here. The shelf with the rat cage is right next to my nose."

Alyssa ignored her aunt's complaint. "You're as bad as they are. You thought you could get me to talk. Well, guess what? The joke's on you. I'm not lying. I don't have a secret."

"But I do," Charlotte said ominously. "This is your last chance, sweetheart. If we put our heads together, we might figure this out. I can tell you about the contacts I made with Frankie."

"From ten years ago," Rafe said. "I expect we'll find that half of them are in jail and the others are dead."

"He's right," Alyssa said. "You don't have much to bargain with. Who are you working for, Charlotte? It is Davidoff?"

"Not a chance. That bastard crossed a line, and I can't forgive him. He's evil to the core."

Alyssa wondered what Davidoff could have done to exceed her aunt's very minimal threshold for bad behavior. Charlotte didn't have a problem with stealing, cheating and deception. Nor did she seem worried about Jessop getting beaten so badly that he had to go to the hospital. Did she draw the line at murder?

"Suppose I agree to work with you," Alyssa said. "Where would we start?"

"It's obvious. We need to sit down with your old buddy Max Horowitz."

Alyssa was glad they were in a dark closet where panic couldn't be seen on her face. The raucous noise from the other room covered the guilty tremor in her voice. "Mr. Horowitz disappeared. Why do you think I'd know where he is?"

"You're closer to him than anyone else."

And she couldn't betray him, couldn't even tell Rafe about the phone call she'd made less than an hour ago. "I don't know where he's hiding." *That much was true.* "And I can't think of a single logical reason he'd steal from his own pawnshop." *Also true.*

"I'll give you a tidbit of information for free," Charlotte said. "There's a forger in Chicago who has information about a murder. It's all about the paint. I've known about this for a couple of months, but I couldn't go to the authorities. You can."

"This cryptic thing doesn't work for me," Alyssa said. "Just tell me."

"Later," Charlotte said. "I've got to run. Goodbye, sweetheart."

"Wait," Rafe said. "The plan was for all three of us to leave together. We can drop you off at a hotel or at the airport."

"Plans change." She shoved her way past them to the front of the closet, stepped into the back room of the shop and shuddered from head to toe. "This place stinks. All that weird stuff in jars gives me the creeps."

As Alyssa watched her aunt stride toward the rear door of the shop, she wondered if she'd ever see the woman again. In memory, she flashed back to a summer day in Chicago when she was nine or ten. Her mom and Charlotte had just finished a set of tennis and were both wearing whites. She'd thought they looked like angels. "Goodbye, Aunt Charlotte."

Alyssa retreated into the closet with Rafe. Now that they were alone, she didn't hesitate to snuggle against his chest. His arms draped over her shoulders, and he pulled her closer. His warmth comforted her. She couldn't hear the beating of his heart over the loud drumming and chanting from the other room, but she felt his vitality and his pulse. While they'd been apart, she was terrified of losing him.

Gently, he kissed her forehead, probably not intending to be sexy, but her engine was already revved. After they'd made love, she couldn't go back to the way it was before when they were merely friends. They were lovers. He knew the secrets of her body and vice versa.

Taking advantage of that knowledge, she went up on her tiptoes and nuzzled against a sensitive place on his throat just beside his carotid artery. He gave a low moan that only she could hear.

"A question, *cher*. Why are we still in the closet?"

"Jolene said to stay until she gave the signal, and she has a very long snake." She kissed his throat again. "She understands reptiles. It only took a minute for her to pick Woodbridge out of the crowd."

"The blood on his shoes was a clue."

"What's our plan?"

"I suggest that we leave here, get into the car and return to the safe house."

More specifically, they'd return to his bed at the safe house. "Here's what worries me. How did Woodbridge know we were here? Did he follow you?"

"It's possible." He shrugged. "After we found Jessop, we had to wait for paramedics and didn't have time to plan a careful exit. We went down the fire escape, a messy retreat. He could have seen us."

She was beginning to know Rafe well enough that she could read between the lines. There was something he wasn't telling her. "Any other theory?"

"I suspect Charlotte is hooked into a tracking device, either voluntarily or someone slipped it into her handbag. Previously, I thought Jessop was monitoring her, but Woodbridge and his cohorts might be the ones keeping tabs on her."

"Too complicated." She nibbled at his throat, tasting the salty flavor of his skin. "I wish I had a scorecard that told me who was playing on which team."

Aunt Charlotte seemed adamant about hating Davidoff, but she was a liar.

If Jessop was Davidoff's contact in New Orleans, why was he beaten? Maybe Woodbridge was working for somebody else, like the Leones in Florida.

The Russian bride of Ray McGill might want revenge against Alyssa for her testimony against her sleazebag husband.

"In the future," she said, "I'll stick to juggling numbers. They're not as complicated as people. By the way, how did you know to go around to the back entrance to the shop?"

"Sheila Marie and I have been texting."

"She's wonderful. Whatever you pay her as a confidential informant, it's not enough. And I like Jolene, as well. Has she ever given you a reading?"

"Many times. After I left the FBI, she predicted a long journey across water and great wealth. What did she tell you?"

She hesitated, not wanting to confess her link to Mr. Horowitz but wanting to be completely transparent with Rafe. "There was something about a tall, dark, handsome man."

"I'm tall and dark. Two out of three is not so bad. *C'est moi!*"

He was also undeniably handsome, but she didn't need to tell him. Rafe had a healthy ego. Her thoughts were interrupted by what sounded like a door being opened. Had Charlotte forgotten to lock it before she abandoned them? "Did you hear that?"

He peeked through the partially open closet door. "It's Woodbridge. He has a gun."

And the closet was the most obvious hiding place. After a cursory look at the rest of the back room, he would surely open this door and find them. They were in big trouble.

But then she had an idea. Woodbridge was afraid of snakes. Maybe rats would have the same effect. She took the mesh cage off the shelf and tried to squeeze past Rafe. "Let me by. This will freak him out."

"What are you doing? Setting free the rats?"

"Yep."

"If we were in a cartoon, I would agree to your plan." With his gun in one hand and his phone in the other, he peeked through the slit in the door. "Stay behind me."

Her adrenaline was already pumping, and her pulse raced. Her rational mind told her that she should be terrified. When Woodbridge opened that door, he'd start firing. Rafe would be forced to do the same. Either way, the result was a bloodbath. She ought to be scared to death, but she wasn't. She believed they'd get through this. Maybe the gris-gris protected her, or maybe she trusted Rafe. She tugged at his sleeve. "What's Woodbridge doing out there?"

"Poking around, touching things, handling the beads and jewelry. He keeps checking a small electronic device and looking toward the front of the shop."

"A tracking device that Charlotte was carrying?"

"That's my best guess."

The atmosphere shifted. The rhythm of the chants sped up, and the volume turned up to high. Alyssa heard Sheila Marie shout, "Look here!"

She must have charged through the bamboo curtain. She continued, "People, do you see? The thief is here. He be stealing our treasures with his bloody hands."

Jolene joined in. "The sacred serpent sees all. Her poison will make his fingers wither into stumps, and he will die."

Alyssa appreciated the drama of Jolene's threat, even though she knew for a fact that Burmese pythons weren't venomous. No doubt Jolene was parading around with her favorite companion, Dominique, held high over her head. Alyssa heard the sounds of people running and dancing and drumming and singing.

"This is hot as the devil's fire," Sheila Marie shouted.

Alyssa thought of the mystery stew boiling on the hot plate. "What's she doing?"

"She's got a pot, and she's getting ready to throw whatever is in it." There was a scream.

Rafe continued, "That was Woodbridge. He's running. A sensible move."

She heard the back door slam.

"The thief is gone," Jolene announced. "Come with me to the front. We will speak of the future and the past and these precious moments in between."

The crowd followed her instructions, which—Alyssa suspected—would lead to readings along with the sale of gris-gris and love potions. She looked up at Rafe and said, "This is the most amazing hideout."

"When I'm here, I never know what to expect."

Sheila Marie opened the closet door. "You okay?"

"How did you know that we needed help?" Alyssa asked.

"The magic of my cell phone. It is not as exotic as voodoo but more efficient. Your tall, handsome man sent a text." She tapped Rafe on the chest and pulled Alyssa out of the closet. "How come you're holding the rats?"

"I thought that if I released them from the cage, they might run after the bad guy."

"Attack rats?"

"It's not like I gave them tiny guns and helmets." She returned the rats to the shelf in the closet. "I like your way better. It sounded like you scared Woodbridge half to death."

"He won't be showing his ugly mug around here again."

Rafe gave her a hug and thanked her. "Give my love to Jolene. We'd better go while Wood-bridge is still too scared to tiptoe into the voo-doo shops."

On the street, she stuck to him like a shadow as he dodged the light and kept to the dark-ness. "We're almost to the car," he said. "I found parking on the street."

She couldn't wait to sink into the comfortable seat of the Mercedes, sit back and ride to the safe house. Only a few days ago, she'd risked her life trying to escape from Rafe. Now she thought of the house as her home, the place where they were surrounded by security and no one could find them.

Why had they left that sweet little nest? Oh yeah, they'd ventured out to warn her aunt that Davidoff was on his way to New Orleans, which was definitely the right thing to do, even though Charlotte hadn't paid much attention and had left them in the lurch.

They rounded a corner. Rafe took two steps and came to a dead halt.

"What's wrong?"

He gestured to an open space at the curb. "Your aunt stole my Mercedes."

Chapter Nineteen

Fuming, Rafe stared at the empty space where the Mercedes should have been waiting for him. There were no words sufficient for his rage. *I trusted that woman. I saved her from being arrested by NOPD.* And this was his payback?

He clasped Alyssa's arm and pulled her off the sidewalk into a nearby alley. Halfway down, he ducked into a darkened doorway, where they wouldn't be seen. His chest was tight, and his lungs constricted. He inhaled a gulp of night air, thick with humidity. Garbage from the seafood restaurant at the front of the alley reeked of onions and fish guts.

There had to be some mistake! He felt around in the pockets of his windbreaker and his jeans, searching for the key fob needed to start the Mercedes. He found his own keys, his Swiss Army knife, an extra clip for his Glock, his wallet and his phone, but the fob for Chance's car was gone. While they'd been jammed in the closet together, Charlotte must have picked his pocket—a skill he wasn't surprised to learn that she possessed.

"I guess we need a new plan," Alyssa said with a grin that was too cheerful for his current mood. "We could hop onto a streetcar and go back to the house."

He hated that solution. Trapped inside a streetcar, they were vulnerable to Woodbridge and the men he was working with. Rafe knew there would be more thugs out on the street, looking for them. Even if Woodbridge had started the evening on his own, he would have summoned backup when he knew their location.

"No streetcars," he said.

"Maybe we can stay in the voodoo shop for the night," she suggested.

For a moment, Rafe considered returning to the Dragon's Blood and lying low, allowing Jolene's python to protect them. But he didn't want to bring more trouble to her doorstep. One encounter was enough.

"I've got a plan," he said darkly. "A simple plan."

She looked up at him expectantly. "What is it?"

He could track down Charlotte and tap her on the shoulder. When she turned around, he could drill a neat bullet hole into the center of her forehead. Ha! The plan gave him momentary relief. She deserved retribution. She'd put them in danger. Right now, she was probably at the airport buying a ticket to an unknown destination. But of course, he wouldn't take such drastic revenge. "Never mind."

Alyssa's eyes were bright. Her attitude determined. In spite of the constant threat and betrayal by her aunt, she remained hopeful. He doubted that she thought of herself as courageous, but the description was apt. He needed to focus and to find the best way to protect her.

"Here's another plan," he said. "Where do you keep your getaway car?"

"A long-term parking structure over by the docks." She pumped her fist like the winner of a tennis match. "I knew that car was going to come in handy."

"Do you have the key?"

She bobbed her head. "In my backpack, I've got the car key and the card to get into and out of the parking garage. I'm so happy we're going to get it. I can really use all the clothes and shoes packed in the trunk."

"I'm guessing that you selected a parking garage that stayed open late."

"Twenty-four-hour access, and there are two night watchmen on duty." She beamed a radiant smile that lit up the dingy alley. "I know which streetcars to take to get there. We'd only need one transfer."

Hadn't he already told her that he wasn't going to hop onto a streetcar like a schoolboy headed to classes? "We'll take a taxi. With all the hotels around here, it won't be hard to find one."

Hand in hand, they walked to the end of the alley. Before they stepped into the comparative light of the street, she pulled her cap down on her forehead—a minimal disguise but better than nothing. All he could do was hunch his shoulders to look shorter and blend in with the other people on the street.

He glanced across the street, looking for the people who were looking for them. In this touristy area, most of the pedestrians were walking in couples or groups. The car traffic on the narrow streets of the French Quarter was minimal, limited mostly to taxis and rickshaws and scooters. The lack of vehicles suited Rafe very well. With the glare from neon streetlights bouncing off windshields, it was difficult to see the interior of a car.

She nudged his shoulder. "Lighten up. You're supposed to be a happy tourist."

Taking on that undercover role, he splashed a smile onto his face. "Do you think we should pretend to be lovers?"

"Pretend?" She threw her arm around his neck and pulled him down for a kiss. "Was that convincing?"

"That was a start."

Though he enjoyed the sensations that came when her body pressed against his, Rafe maintained his surveillance. He noticed two men standing at the street corner who didn't cross when the light changed from red to green. One of them spoke into a phone. The other wore sunglasses.

Smoothly, he guided Alyssa into an open storefront packed with colorful souvenirs: post-cards, scarves and T-shirts. He pretended to admire a bottle of Tabasco sauce. "Check out the men on the corner."

"I see them. Sunglasses at night are a dumb disguise." She dangled a string of Mardi Gras beads from her fingers. "They're just standing there, not moving."

"We should double back."

They didn't have to wait for a distraction. A casual four-piece brass band, including a tuba, marched down the sidewalk, pausing to give a shout every few steps. *Gotta love New Orleans*. Rafe tugged her hand, and they went back the way they'd come.

Though he didn't actually see Woodbridge, he felt the pursuit as surely as a chipmunk senses the approach of a hawk. On these streets, people were watching them and listening for the sound of their voices. They needed to escape the French Quarter.

Rafe directed their route closer to the Bourbon Street hotels, where he had no problem hailing a black-and-white cab. He told the driver to take them to Louis Armstrong Airport. When the cabbie—a woman with curly red hair and a derby hat—set out, he watched through the back window, trying to spot suspicious characters on the street and the sidewalk.

"Why are we going to the airport?" she asked. "Are you going to look for Charlotte?"

He was still too angry to face that woman. "I want to get away from the crowd in the French Quarter. On the open road, we'll be able to see if we're being followed. I expect to change cabs at least twice more before we go to your parking facility."

In his mind, he laid out a grid of the city, fitting together the unique parishes of New Orleans like pieces of a puzzle. In addition to the residential streets and areas dedicated to business and commerce, there were historic structures and government buildings. Throughout this map of irregular shapes were slivers of the tourism industry, restaurants, art venues and an amazing selection of music, ranging from smooth jazz to Samoan war chants. Visitors had a wide choice of activity, and the people who lived here had it all.

He gazed through the window as the streets unfolded around him. His city. He never wanted to leave again. Somehow, he needed to convince Alyssa to stay here with him.

After reversing their route to the airport, he directed their taxi to the neighborhood around Tulane, where he'd grown up, then to a Marriott on Canal Street. Anyone following them would be confused. The red-haired taxi driver told him that he was *couyon*, crazy.

He heard Alyssa's ringtone. She took her phone from her backpack and checked the identification. "Anonymous," she said. "It's not the same number Charlotte had before, but I'll bet it's her."

He agreed. When Charlotte stole the Mercedes, she had recommitted to her life on the run. The first thing she needed was a new disposable phone. "Put her on speaker."

Alyssa answered. "Who's this?"

"I need to explain something," Charlotte said.

"If you're planning to make some kind of lame excuse for taking the car, don't bother. That was just plain wrong. It's not even our car."

"I'll get the car back to you."

Rafe didn't believe a word that woman said,

not a word. He could have warned her that Chance was the kind of guy who had electronic alerts installed on his Mercedes. At the stroke of a few computer keys, he'd know her location.

"Are you at the airport?" Alyssa asked. "We could come and pick you up."

Slowly, Rafe shook his head from side to side. *No more favors for Auntie Charlotte.*

"Listen to me," Charlotte said. "Remember when I told you about that forger who had evidence about a murder?"

"I remember."

"This evidence is actually one of the reasons I wanted to find you in New Orleans. It's important, sweetheart. I guess I should start by telling you that this guy isn't a great forger, but he's an excellent tattoo artist."

"How would you know?" Alyssa asked.

"I've had some work done. There's an angel on my heart and a butterfly on my bottom. Also, this guy has a reputation for doing amazing custom paint jobs on fancy cars."

Rafe felt himself being drawn in to her story. Angry as he was at Alyssa's aunt, he admired her ability to spin a web of deceit. She'd have made a good undercover operative.

"This artist," Charlotte said, "came into possession of a couple of paint chips from a custom job on a Beamer that had been in an accident.

The front end was all caved in. At the time, my artist friend was working in a chop shop where they break down stolen cars and—"

"I know what a chop shop is," Alyssa interrupted.

"So you understand when I tell you that the car was completely refurbished and is unidentifiable as having been in a hit-and-run accident."

Like the accident that killed her mother. The blood drained from Alyssa's face. Her arm went limp, and Rafe scooped the phone off the seat of the taxi. Alyssa stared straight ahead, clearly devastated.

If this was some kind of scam, he'd have to revisit his revenge fantasy about shooting Charlotte. He kept his voice low. "What else do you know?"

"By the way, Rafe, I really do feel bad about taking off with the Mercedes."

He didn't believe her. "Tell me about the paint chip."

"I can do better than tell you," she said. "Is Alyssa all right?"

"She's in shock."

"I'm glad you're with her. She needs someone to support her."

He wasn't going to let himself get thrown off track by Charlotte's phony concern. "When did the tattoo artist find this paint chip?"

"About five years ago."

That fit the time frame for her mother's death. "Where did he find it?"

"The chop shop belongs to Diamond Jim. I can't say for sure who was driving, but Davidoff has information that I'm guessing he never shared with the police."

In itself, a paint chip—even an exact match to the hit-and-run vehicle—didn't prove anything. "I need more information."

"How about this for a headline—Alyssa has the chip. It's in a plastic baggie, and I tucked it into her backpack. That's why I called. I didn't want her to accidentally throw it out."

She still wasn't telling him everything. Pulling information from her was harder than wrenching a snack from the jaws of a snapping turtle. "Why do you believe this is evidence?"

"I forgot the most important part." With some frustration, he imagined her sly, Cheshire cat grin. She was playing with him. "There's blood on the paint chips. I didn't have a way to test DNA, but if someone had friends in law enforcement, they might get those tests done, which would give the identity of the victim."

And provide a link between Davidoff's chop shop and the victim of a hit-and-run from five years ago... Alyssa's mom. "That's good stuff."

"Damn right," she said.

"I might have to forgive you, after all."

"Essentially, I'm a good person. Give my niece a big hug and keep me posted." She made kissy noises. "Adieu, Rafe."

"*Au revoir*, crazy lady."

He gathered Alyssa in his arms and held her without speaking while he sent the cabbie on another wild ride through the Treme parish and up to Gentilly. The music from the radio was oldies and Elvis. The ride wasn't unpleasant.

Finally, Alyssa spoke. "I should be pleased. I might find out who killed my mom. But I feel… empty."

"You need time to think," he said. "Here's a new plan. Instead of hanging around in the city, trying to piece together clues while the bad guys are after us, we leave town. From a distance, I might be able to work with my FBI contacts and find someone we can trust."

She nodded. "Maybe that's for the best."

After returning to Canal Street, they disembarked, picked up another ride and went on a circuitous route before switching to yet another cab outside another hotel in the central business district. Tucked into the rear of that taxi, he kissed her cheek. "Are we close to your parking garage?"

"Less than a mile away." With her thumb, she stroked the leather surface of the voodoo gris-gris. Her eyelids drooped, and she yawned. "I'm so tired."

He might have pushed her too hard. "If you want, we can stay at this hotel."

"I'd rather get this done." She sat up straight and shook herself. "We have a plan, and I want to follow through."

In the warehouse district near the docks, they left the taxi outside a parking garage with a straggly palm tree and a vertical neon sign that said Park. The homely four-story blond-brick structure with windows marching in horizontal lines on each floor reminded him of her storage warehouse near Café du Monde.

He asked, "Do you have a thing for ugly brick buildings?"

"I spent most of my life in cities, so I guess the answer is yes."

"What does the garage look like inside?"

"Totally organized. The exit ramp is in the middle, and cars are parked on each side. Mine is on the fourth floor." She pointed to the double entrance and exit with wooden arms blocking each side. "The night watchman's booth is over there. We need to check in with him."

She paused to dig through her backpack, mumbling something about her alias for this garage. "Don't call me Alyssa or Lara. This car is in the name of Wanda Wilson. I need to show her ID to the guard."

"The name doesn't fit, *cher.* I think of Wanda as a taller woman, maybe a blonde."

"You're wrong," she said. "When I choose my aliases, I usually stick to something related. Lara is short for Larissa, which sounds like Alyssa, which led to another fake name of Alice. Wanda came to me by surprise. I don't have friends or family named Wanda, don't know anybody named Wanda. Wanda Wilson reminds me of a mermaid. Am I babbling?"

"A bit."

"I'm excited, Rafe. This is almost over, which means we have a chance to try a normal life." She hesitated. "Is that something you want?"

He didn't think life with Lara/Larissa/Alyssa/Wanda would ever be considered normal. "When this is over, I want to be with you. We don't need a label. It doesn't have to be normal or exotic or anything else. Just you and me."

She planted a quick kiss on his mouth then dug deeper into her pack and pulled out the plastic baggie containing the precious chip of evidence. "It's hard to believe this little scrap of old paint could change my life. I want you to hold on to it, then you can give it to your DNA people."

The chip had been protected by bubble wrap

before being placed in an envelope and tucked into the baggie for safekeeping. He tucked the small package into the inner jacket of his windbreaker, hoping it could actually be useful as evidence. Off the top of his head, he could think of dozens of reasons a defense attorney would object to a paint chip that had been passed from one person to the next without maintaining chain of evidence. But it was a starting point for reopening the investigation.

Retrieving her Chevy station wagon presented no particular problems. The twelve-year-old vehicle didn't have the horsepower or the luxury suspension of the Mercedes, but it was a decent ride. He drove carefully onto the city streets. At this hour on a Sunday night, the traffic was light, and he was ninety-nine percent sure that they weren't being followed. "I'm tempted to get on the highway right now."

"We need to wait until morning when I can go to the bank," she said. "I need the cash and credit cards from my safe-deposit box…and the thumb drive."

Though he wasn't anxious to pursue the investigation any further, he knew she wouldn't be safe until they found the missing millions. "We'll go early tomorrow, *à demain*."

When he drove the Chevy onto the street where the safe house was located, he didn't feel the sense of relief that usually accompanied a return to home base. A lamp in the front room was lit, and the porch light was on. That was the way he'd left the house, and he hadn't received any security alerts on his phone.

He parked on the breezeway and unlocked the back door. As soon as he stepped inside, he smelled freshly brewed coffee. Something was wrong.

Alyssa charged past him. "I should unload some of the boxes from the car, but that can wait. Right now, I want to rest."

He turned on an overhead light in the kitchen.

Three men with guns drawn stood in the corners of the room. They had the drop on him. He couldn't react without putting Alyssa in mortal danger.

Sitting at the kitchen table, and cradling a mug of coffee in his beefy hands, was Viktor Davidoff.

Chapter Twenty

Her heart stopped beating. Alyssa felt her lungs shut down. Drained of strength, her arms and legs went limp, and yet she remained standing, held in place by invisible strings while she stared into the face of the man who had probably killed her mother. She barely knew Davidoff, had only met him once or twice before. He hadn't made much of an impression on her. Though his grooming was sheer perfection from his shaved head to his neatly trimmed black goatee and tailored suit, he had the rough, thick hands of a peasant farmer.

His lips were moving. He seemed to be talking, but the inside of her head filled with a static buzz, and she couldn't hear his words. *I have to answer, can't just stand and wait for these people to kill me. I have to be smart.*

Desperately, she wanted to survive, to escape this situation in one piece and bring Rafe along with her. After all they'd been through, they deserved a chance.

She inhaled a huge gasp of air and immediately started coughing. Trying to keep from falling, she grabbed the back of one of the kitchen chairs and collapsed onto the seat. A glass of water appeared on the table in front of her. She took a sip and looked over the rim at the man who sat opposite her. He wore a dark blue suit with a yellow ascot fastened in place with a flashy piece of jewelry—a diamond pin for Diamond Jim. His wristwatch was platinum. He wore one large ring on each hand, probably to inflict maximum damage when he was beating on some poor soul who dared to cross him.

She forced herself to keep looking at him, hiding her disdain. He didn't deserve pretty things. This man had played a part in killing her mother—he didn't deserve to live. Dark thoughts hammered inside her skull. She hated him, wanted revenge. Whatever she had to do, she was ready. He wasn't going to beat her.

"I almost fainted." She kept her tone low, soft and nonthreatening. Since she didn't have the power to threaten Davidoff, she wanted to get inside his head. "I was shocked to see you, surprised and happy."

Like a grizzly bear watching his prey, he

cocked his head to one side and focused intently. "Explain yourself, girl."

She glanced over her shoulder at Rafe, who was handcuffed with armed guards on either side of him. Anger clenched inside her, but she pushed it aside. "Please don't be upset with my bodyguard. He didn't mean to tell your secret, but I begged. I can be very persuasive."

"What is this secret?" Davidoff demanded.

"You know," she said, daring to be flirtatious. Her ploy was to be cute and seductive and make him like her enough to let her and Rafe live, at least until morning. "All my life, I've dreamed of this moment when I'd meet the man my mom loved so much that she left her beloved home in Savannah and moved to Chicago. I can't wait to get to know you, Father."

One of his thugs grunted in apparent disbelief, and she bolted to her feet to confront him. "You don't believe me? Well, let me show you the room he arranged exactly the way I like it. My father was worried about me. He hired a full-time bodyguard. That's true, isn't it?"

"She is correct," Davidoff said.

Gritting her teeth so she wouldn't vomit, she took a step closer to him. "May I embrace you, Father?"

He opened his arms. "Come to me."

When she touched him, her stomach curdled.

Not only was the man a disgusting liar, but he wore too much aftershave. "Now that you're here," she said, "we can work together to find the missing millions."

"And how will we accomplish that?"

"Rafe can tell you our plan," she said. "Please take off the handcuffs."

Davidoff gestured, and his minions did as he indicated. The cuffs were removed, and Rafe was welcomed to the kitchen table. If there hadn't been three men with guns plus Davidoff, she thought Rafe might have lashed out. But he was smarter than that. In a few words, he explained how they needed to go to her safe-deposit box at the bank and compare her accounting data with the other information they had.

"What was your source for the original data?" Davidoff asked.

"Let's just say that I still have friends in the FBI."

"Friends like Jessop?"

"He was on your payroll," Rafe said. "Now he's in the hospital."

"Not on my orders," Davidoff said. "I was pleased with Jessop. He's a skilled agent, and there's always room for such a person in my organization. He managed to do the impossible and find this safe house."

"How?" Rafe asked bluntly.

She knew how proud Rafe was of his supposedly impregnable security. He had to be curious about how Davidoff and his thugs had found this place and managed to get inside without setting off the alarms. When she recalled the events of the day, she realized that Rafe's first encounter with Jessop was at the cemetery. Could he have planted a tracking device on Rafe's SUV? Even if he had, it wouldn't matter because they'd left that car with Chance before they returned to the house. If not a tracking device, then what?

She spoke up. "Can I guess?"

"You?" Davidoff sounded amused. "A pretty girl like you has no need to know about equipment and electronics."

"The way you bypassed security has to do with Rafe's phone," she said. "Jessop figured out how to break through the protective firewalls and read the security system on Rafe's phone."

Rafe groaned. "He cloned me. The FBI has been working on this technology for years. When Jessop was near my phone in the cemetery, he transferred my data to another phone."

"A clone," she said.

Davidoff reached over and patted her cheek in a parental gesture that would have been sweet if he really had been her long-lost father. "You're very bright," he said.

"I must take after you, Father."

"Call me Papa."

She suppressed her revulsion. "You're too kind, Papa."

"I found you in time," he said, claiming all the credit. "I saved you."

Apparently, Woodbridge and his thugs—the guys who beat up Jessop—were part of another faction. She needed to get away from Davidoff, needed to have time alone with Rafe to plan their escape. She stretched her arms over her head. "I'm so tired. May I go to bed, Papa?"

"Of course, my dear one. We can take care of the safe-deposit box in the morning."

Now came the tricky part. She decided on the brazen approach, taking Rafe's hand and giving a proprietary tug. "Come on," she said to him. "We should get some sleep."

"Not in the same room," Davidoff said.

"But, Papa, I like him. I mean, I really like him." She was shocked by her innate ability to act like a spoiled daughter. Was teenaged whining part of her DNA? "You want me to be happy, don't you?"

"I will decide if this man is good for you. Now, off to bed."

One of the thugs escorted her down the hall toward her bedroom. She had to stop in the bathroom first, where she locked the door, went to the toilet and puked. She was playing a dangerous game, and the stakes were literally life or death.

She splashed water on her face and looked at herself in the mirror over the sink. Her panic wasn't readily apparent, and she wondered if her DNA also included some of the deceit that made Charlotte such a good liar.

Alyssa needed an edge. She took out her phone and punched in the secret number for Mr. Horowitz. When the mechanical voice answered, she whispered the address of the safe house into the receiver. "Davidoff is holding me and Rafe here." She rattled off the address. "I need your help. Please."

He had to respond. Mr. Horowitz was her only chance.

As soon as Alyssa left the room, Davidoff turned toward Rafe. Stroking his goatee with his full lips curved in an evil grin, he looked like a villain from the old-fashioned movies his mama used to watch. Rafe missed his family; they would have liked Alyssa.

"You didn't tell me about the data she has hidden in her safe-deposit box," Davidoff said. "And you neglected to mention that you and Alyssa are intimate. These things seem disloyal, Rafe. I'm your employer."

"My relationship with her is very much to your advantage," Rafe said.

"How so?"

After Alyssa's Oscar-winning performance as the prodigal daughter, he needed to present a cover story of his own. Davidoff would never believe that he was a minion, but he might be able to work a deal. "If she trusts me and knows that I trust you, she'll cooperate. If you had told me from the start about the money, I might have gotten further with her instead of following her around for two weeks."

"You would have taken the millions for yourself," Davidoff said as he pushed the coffee mug away. "Where do you keep the vodka?"

"I don't actually live in this house. And I don't entertain."

"No vodka? I'll take care of it." He snapped his pudgy fingers at a very large man with an equally huge weapon. "Two bottles. We'll toast to our success in retrieving the money I lost at the pawnshop warehouse and the profit I will earn."

When Rafe reviewed Alyssa's work on the information Chance had given her, he'd noticed several expensive cars unaccounted for. "You lost a Lamborghini V12 when Frankie Leone was killed. That must have hurt."

"What do you know of cars?"

It was the perfect opening. Rafe slipped into his undercover identity as a former Grand Prix race car driver. They talked until the vodka came. And then they talked some more.

When they were three shots into the bottle, Davidoff pinned him with an icy stare and said, "I like you, Rafe. I'll be sorry if I have to kill you."

Chapter Twenty-One

In spite of her fears and anger, Alyssa managed to sleep. It helped that she'd convinced one of Davidoff's minions to bring in her suitcase from the car, and she had a soft, comfortable nightshirt to wear in bed.

When her mattress bounced, she awakened instantly. If this was one of Davidoff's boys, she'd have to beat him to death with her crystal potpourri bowl. She heard murmuring and the word *cher*. There was only one person who called her that. "Rafe?"

"C'est moi." When he stretched out in the bed beside her, she couldn't believe it was really him. He smelled like booze. "You've been drinking."

"That's the vodka, *cher*." He got very close to her ear and said, "Gotta be careful. Watch out for hidden microphones and cameras."

"I found two devices, one under the table lamp and another on the dresser."

"Look at you, being so smart." He planted a sloppy kiss on her cheek. "Can I turn on the lamp? I want to see your pretty face."

"Does Davidoff know you're here?"

"I told him I was going to the bathroom." He turned on the light and gazed down at her. "You're beautiful, the most beautiful woman in the world."

"Do you still have your phone?" she asked. "In case I need to call you?"

"Nope, Davidoff took my cloned phone." He repeated the words. "Cloned phone, cloned phone. I wish I'd remembered that technology before I got within twenty yards of Jessop."

"You should leave before we get caught."

"I want to spend every minute with you. We don't have much time left."

This wasn't what she needed to hear. Alyssa was already disgusted with herself for pretending to be the daughter of a man she hated, a monster. But she'd been feeling that things were under control. "Does he know I'm…"

He shushed her before she could finish the sentence. "They could be listening."

"True."

"He's a businessman," Rafe said. "It's all about the bottom line."

"So if we find the money for him, he'll let us go."

He got close to her ear again. "If we deliver, he has no more use for us. On the other hand, we're expendable if we fail. A classic case of damned if we do and damned if we don't."

"How do we get out of this?"

"Look for a miracle," he said.

"That's not reassuring."

"It could happen. For example, what are the odds of a woman like you and a man like me getting together? Yet, here we are. When it comes to Davidoff and these guys who work for him, we stay alert and wait for something to turn up. Then we take advantage."

He swept her into his arms for a deep, passionate kiss that was better than she expected, given the amount of vodka he'd been drinking. Then he staggered to his feet and went out the door, leaving her with miserable thoughts about her own mortality. *Wait for a miracle.* Not the most useful advice—she needed specifics. Did miracles carry guns? Would the cavalry come riding over the hill?

Again, she took out her phone. This time, she sent a text to Mr. Horowitz with the address of the safe house and pertinent information. Why hadn't he answered her? He was her only chance, and he wasn't paying attention. She didn't want to imagine that something bad might have happened to him. She couldn't bear to lose another person she loved.

THE NEXT MORNING, Alyssa showered and dressed in a beige linen suit for her trip to the bank. Though she had the platform sandals that went with the outfit, she opted for more comfortable loafers that would be good for running. Instead of taking her huge backpack, she put selected items in a much smaller shoulder bag that contained her phone, her wallet with the necessary identification in her current name, keys and miscellaneous things, like lotion, sunglasses, a notepad and pen.

In the kitchen, Davidoff greeted her with a cup of coffee. "Not chicory," he said. "I hate that stuff."

Rafe sat at the kitchen table. In spite of his bloodshot eyes and stubble that was beginning to look like a beard, he was cool and handsome. He greeted her quietly.

In contrast, Davidoff boomed, "Your boyfriend can't handle his vodka."

She took advantage of another opportunity to remind Davidoff of their supposed connection. "He's not Russian, Papa. He's not like us."

He patted her shoulder. "You're a good girl."

"Are we going to the bank this morning?"

"Very soon," he said. "I'll go inside with you.

After you open your box and take out the contents, we'll return to the car and come back here."

"I'm frightened," she said. "Do you know what happened to the guys who were after me, the ones who beat up on Jessop?"

"You have no need to worry. My men will protect you."

She tried a different tactic. "I'd feel a lot better if Rafe came along."

"You must be brave, little sparrow." His grin looked sinister, as though he'd just tasted something unpleasant. "Let's go. Take your coffee."

Before leaving, she gazed at Rafe, trying to communicate silently and tell him that she wasn't giving up hope. Something miraculous would turn up.

She and Davidoff sat in the back of a vintage Lincoln Town Car—a spacious, gorgeous vehicle. Two of his henchmen were in the front: one was the driver and the other held his semiautomatic weapon on his lap. She considered jumping out of the moving car but decided against it. If she ran, Rafe would pay the price.

While Davidoff talked about New Orleans as though he knew his way around this complicated city, she gazed at him with the kind of adoration a daughter reserves for her father. She nodded and smiled at every dopey thing he said.

How was she going to escape? How could she get a message to the authorities?

At the bank in the central business district, they entered the dimly lit underground parking lot. Davidoff ordered his men to wait and then took her arm to escort her. She could feel the endgame approaching. Her pulse accelerated, and she began to sweat.

"You're trembling," Davidoff said.

"I told you I was scared."

"You'll be fine. I will be standing close beside you."

And that was the problem. She didn't want him anywhere near her. If she could put some distance between them, she might make a break for it. Her opportunity came when the bank official—a tall, lean black man with an officious manner—escorted her into the private room beside the safe-deposit vaults.

"I'll leave you alone," the official said. "If you need help, my name is Mr. Morgan."

Davidoff was right behind him. "I need to get into the room with her."

"I'm sorry, sir. That's against our rules."

"Your damn rules must be changed."

While Mr. Morgan called his supervisor for permission, she took the notepad from her shoulder bag and scribbled three words: *I'm. Being. Kidnapped.*

There was no time for more explanation. As soon as Morgan opened the door, Davidoff charged into the private room, roaring like a bull. Though she tried to placate him, he wasn't accustomed to having his will thwarted. Quickly, she emptied her box into a shopping bag she'd brought for the purpose.

As they left the room, she pressed the note into Mr. Morgan's hand, and she almost got away with it. Her miracle crashed and burned when Davidoff pounced. He snatched the small scrap of paper, opened it, read it and turned his large, shaved head toward her. "This is not funny, little sparrow."

"I wasn't making a joke."

"Please excuse her," he said to Morgan. This time when he grabbed her arm, his grip tightened like a vise. "Don't try any other stunts or Rafe is dead."

She wanted to scream her lungs out, but she couldn't take the chance. There might be a way to talk him back into a good mood.

In the underground parking lot, he slammed her against the rear left fender of the Lincoln. "Why?"

"I want to get away from you. Just let me go."

"But you are my beloved." He sneered. "My long-lost daughter."

"We both know that's a lie. You tried to scam

me but made a mistake. The music box played the wrong tune."

He signaled to the driver. "Open the trunk."

Before she had time to object, the other thug shoved her into the extra-large trunk space and closed the lid. Davidoff issued one more order, and he spoke loudly enough that she could hear.

"Call the house," he said. "Kill Rafe."

RAFE SAT UNCOMFORTABLY on the kitchen chair. After Davidoff left with Alyssa, the two guys who stayed behind replaced his handcuffs so he wouldn't attempt an escape. He watched as the supersize thug took a call. The only word he said repeatedly was "yeah."

He ended the call, gave Rafe a wink and drew his semiautomatic. The bore of the gun barrel pointing at Rafe's belly gaped as wide as a cannon's maw. He hoped death would be fast.

The back door crashed open. Three guys in lace-up boots, helmets and military garb charged inside. Taking advantage of the element of surprise, they disarmed Davidoff's thugs in a few minutes. One of them unlocked Rafe's handcuffs. He had just enough time to stand up before their leader entered.

He was slightly below average height, white-haired with a walrus mustache to match. He wore baggy khakis, a short-sleeved white shirt and a plaid sweater vest. He held out his hand to Rafe and said, "I'm Max Horowitz."

"And I'm Rafe Fournier. Thank you for saving my life."

"Lara mentioned meeting a fellow. Is that you?"

"I hope so," he said.

"Where is she?"

"On her way back from the bank, but she should have been here by now."

Horowitz took his phone from his pocket and punched in a number, leaving the phone on speaker. "I told her to call me if she ran into trouble. She's the only person with this number." Impatiently, he tapped his foot on the kitchen floor. "If she doesn't answer, how will we find her?"

"Mr. Horowitz, is that you?" Her voice was a little choppy.

"It is, and I'm here with Rafe. Where are you?"

"In the trunk of a vintage Lincoln Town Car," she said. "Davidoff is really mad. I've got to get away from him."

"I don't know my way around the city as well as Rafe," Horowitz said, turning to him.

She gave a small cry. "Rafe is still alive! Thank God! Davidoff told them to kill him."

"We'll talk later, *cher*. Do you know where you are?"

"Definitely not headed back to the house. The

driver seems to be lost. I kicked out part of the taillight, and I can see bits of scenery as we go past."

"Tell me what you see."

"We were wandering around by the docks and warehouses. Now the houses look like Treme. We're heading toward Canal Street."

Last night's tour of the city was proving useful. While she described various landmarks, he and Horowitz and two of his three paramilitary guys got into an SUV and tried to follow her directions.

Back and forth and around, it felt like they were on Mister Toad's Wild Ride until she came up with a definitive location. "We're in the Ninth Ward."

"That's a lot of real estate," said one of the men working for Horowitz.

Rafe spoke gently into the phone. "Alyssa, try to see some of the houses. We need more clues to tell us where you are."

"I can't."

She went quiet, and he thought he heard gentle weeping. "Don't give up. It's time for our miracle."

"Purple with yellow stripes," she said. "I remember seeing this house when we were here before. It's not far from the church. And we're stopping."

He barked directions at the guy who was driving, and they whipped through the streets of the Ninth Ward. The big, beautiful Town Car wasn't hard to spot. Was Alyssa still in the trunk? Was she okay?

They approached the location with military precision. Rafe didn't know where Horowitz had found these guys, but they were top-notch. Davidoff and his men weren't expecting an assault and were easily overpowered. Before they had time to react, they were disarmed and cuffed. Their leader flipped open the trunk of the big car, and Alyssa popped up.

When she ran to him and threw her arms around his neck, Rafe had never felt so fulfilled and complete. He wasn't ready to declare his intentions, but he felt love in every fiber of his body. He wanted to be with her forever.

She showered a half dozen kisses on his face. "You told me there would be a miracle. And you were right."

For a few moments, she transferred her affection to Horowitz, who was absolutely delighted to see her. Then she leaped back to Rafe.

Her beige linen suit was ruined after being in the trunk. She had smudges on her cheeks, and her eye makeup was a mess. Still, he thought she was beautiful, prettier than Scarlett O'Hara and all the other southern belles combined.

"Do you know the worst part of this mess?" she asked her two men. "I had to pretend that Davidoff was my father. That could never be. He's a monster."

"You're right," Horowitz said. "I know, because I'm your father."

Rafe wasn't as shocked as he might have been. Max Horowitz had taken care of her for many years, giving her a job and sending her to college. Those considerations went far beyond the duties of an employer. Max had trusted her with his secrets.

The old man reached into his pocket and produced a photograph. "Here's proof."

Alyssa held the picture in both hands. "This is you, but your hair isn't gray. And that's Mom, and she's looking at you like you're her whole world."

He nodded. "That's the way you look at Rafe."

"And the child in the picture?"

"I'm sure you recognize the teddy bear," he said.

"It's mine. Bobo Bear. This is crazy. We look like such a normal family."

"Your mother and I were soulmates. We tried so hard to protect you and make a good life that we lost track of what was truly important. Don't be foolish like we were. Put your love first and foremost, and then everything else will fall into place."

"I agree with every word you say."

"Your father is wise," Rafe said.

She took his hands in hers. "You are my pirate, my bodyguard and my dearest love. I never want to be apart from you again."

He cinched his arm around her slender waist and pulled her close for the first of an eternity of kisses.

Epilogue

Drinking sweetened tea on the veranda outside Chance's plantation home, Rafe finished telling the story to his friend as they watched Alyssa ride across the front field on a prancing Arabian mare. She was laughing with her head thrown back, and she looked like the embodiment of freedom.

"A mostly happy ending," Chance said, "especially since I got my Mercedes back."

"More than mostly happy," Rafe said. "This was perfect. Woodbridge and his friends got picked up by the cops and will rot in jail for many years."

"What about Davidoff?"

"On trial in Chicago," Rafe said. "The paint chip was enough to reopen the investigation into the hit-and-run murder of her mom."

"Here's a big fat flaw in your story—you and Alyssa didn't get your hands on the millions of dollars."

"And neither did anybody else. Frankie Leone had been pilfering little bits and pieces over the years, nowhere near millions. That big payoff never really existed except on paper, which is something Alyssa would have found when she compared the data from her records and the stuff you got on your computer hack. Horowitz set up the lure to draw out a bunch of smugglers. The FBI and ATF moved in and scooped them up."

"I guess you're right," Chance said. "What are you going to do to top this story?"

Rafe took a small box from his pocket and flipped open the lid. "Five carats, flawless, canary yellow."

"Nice. That should lead to another extremely happy ending."

* * * * *

Don't miss The Final Secret,
the previous title from
USA TODAY *bestselling author*
Cassie Miles.
It's available now wherever
Harlequin Intrigue books are sold!

Get 4 FREE REWARDS!

We'll send you 2 FREE Books
plus 2 FREE Mystery Gifts.

Harlequin Romantic Suspense books are heart-racing page-turners with unexpected plot twists and irresistible chemistry that will keep you guessing to the very end.

FREE Value Over **$20**

YES! Please send me 2 FREE Harlequin Romantic Suspense novels and my 2 FREE gifts (gifts are worth about $10 retail). After receiving them, if I don't wish to receive any more books, I can return the shipping statement marked "cancel." If I don't cancel, I will receive 4 brand-new novels every month and be billed just $4.99 per book in the U.S. or $5.74 per book in Canada. That's a savings of at least 13% off the cover price! It's quite a bargain! Shipping and handling is just 50¢ per book in the U.S. and $1.25 per book in Canada.* I understand that accepting the 2 free books and gifts places me under no obligation to buy anything. I can always return a shipment and cancel at any time. The free books and gifts are mine to keep no matter what I decide.

240/340 HDN GNMZ

Name (please print)

Address   Apt. #

City   State/Province   Zip/Postal Code

Email: Please check this box ☐ if you would like to receive newsletters and promotional emails from Harlequin Enterprises ULC and its affiliates. You can unsubscribe anytime.

Mail to the **Reader Service:**
IN U.S.A.: P.O. Box 1341, Buffalo, NY 14240-8531
IN CANADA: P.O. Box 603, Fort Erie, Ontario L2A 5X3

Want to try 2 free books from another series? Call 1-800-873-8635 or visit www.ReaderService.com.